Did you know that in America a grasshopper is sometimes called a katydid because of the noise it makes? Long ago, in 1872, that noise gave Susan Coolidge the idea for a story, and ever since then girls everywhere have loved to read about Katy and her adventures.

British Library Cataloguing in Publication Data

Ainsworth, Alison
    What Katy did.—(Ladybird children's classics. Series no. 740).
    I. Title   II. Coolidge, Susan, *1835-1905*
    III. Tourret, Gwen   IV. Tourret, Pat
    823'.914[J]
    ISBN 0-7214-1117-7

First edition

Published by Ladybird Books Ltd Loughborough Leicestershire UK
Ladybird Books Inc Auburn Maine 04210 USA

© LADYBIRD BOOKS LTD MCMLXXXVIII

Printed in England

WHAT KATY DID

by Susan Coolidge

retold by Alison Ainsworth
illustrated by Gwen and Pat Tourret

Ladybird Books

The Carr family

Katy Carr was twelve years old. She lived in a large white house on the edge of a small town in America.

There were six children in Katy's family — four girls and two boys — and Katy was the oldest. The children's Mama had died when Katy was eight. The children's father, Papa, was a dear, kind man. He was a doctor, and was always busy looking after sick people. Sometimes he was away from home all day, and sometimes half the night.

Papa's sister, Aunt Izzie, had come to take care of the family when Mama died. She wasn't as gentle or as pretty as Mama. She was much older and had a rather sharp face.

Papa liked to see his girls and boys enjoying themselves, playing rough-and-tumble games, but Aunt Izzie wasn't used to boisterous children. She wished they would just sit quietly and read or sew.

But Katy wasn't the sort of girl who *could* sit still for long. She was for ever rushing about, her head full of adventures. Katy was tall for her age, with long hair which never stayed tidy for long. Her best friend, Cecy, was quite the opposite. She was a pretty girl who was always neatly dressed. How Katy longed to be like Cecy! But poor Katy was always getting into trouble, mostly because she was so untidy and careless.

She would often daydream about doing something really brave, like saving a child from drowning. Then she would become famous, and everyone would admire her. Once, when she was only six, Katy found a little girl in the street. Katy thought she must be an orphan. She wanted to look after the little girl, so she took her home and hid her in the attic.

But the 'orphan' was frightened of the dark. In the middle of the night she woke up, screaming. Mama and Papa had to take the poor little girl back to her mother, who had been very worried about her.

Katy's sisters were called Clover, Elsie and Joanna. Clover, who was nearly eleven, was a sweet, plump girl. She had big blue eyes and thick plaits of light brown hair. Katy and Clover were very close.

Elsie was eight years old. She was a thin child with dark eyes and short curly hair. Poor Elsie always seemed to be the odd one out in the family. She was too old to play with the little ones, and Katy and Clover thought her too childish for their 'grown up' games.

Joanna, the youngest of the sisters, was five. She was quite a tomboy. Everyone called her John or Johnnie.

Katy's brothers were Dorry, a pale, solemn boy of six, and Phil, a handsome four year old.

With such a big family to look after, Aunt Izzie certainly had her hands full!

Happy times

On wet days the children would run across the back yard to the barn. In the middle of the barn there was a tall wooden post with steps all the way up. The children climbed up the post to the loft. This was their favourite place to play in wet weather.

The loft was long and low, and quite dark and dusty. There were lots of cobwebs too, but the children didn't mind. They would all sit in a circle while Katy read one of her stories. She was always writing tales of adventure or romance.

Then the children took turns to tell stories of their own, or to sing their favourite songs.

Behind the barn there was a big garden full of vegetables, and a pasture where four cows grazed. The children spent many happy hours there. At the far end of the pasture was a small thicket of trees and bushes. The children called this place *Paradise*. Here they could play to their hearts' content, away from Aunt Izzie's watchful eye.

One sunny Saturday morning the children went to Paradise, to have a picnic. Katy and Cecy led the way and the others followed. Dorry and John were laden with great leafy branches. Katy and Cecy had each been carrying a wicker picnic basket. These they put down in the shade of a large poplar tree. Then they all helped to build a shelter with the branches brought by Dorry and John.

When it was time to eat, the children crowded together in the shelter. Katy opened the picnic baskets. What a feast met their eyes! Aunt Izzie certainly knew how to feed hungry children. She had made two kinds of sandwiches – corned beef and ham – and there were hard-boiled eggs, ginger cakes and cookies. But best of all were seven little molasses pies, each with a crisp sugary top.

How good everything tasted! The fresh wind rustled the leaves, the sun was shining and the birds sang. No grown up dinner party was ever so much fun.

In no time at all every crumb had disappeared. The children licked their sticky fingers. Then they lay in the long cool grass, or climbed into the wide branches of the poplar tree.

How lovely it was to stretch out in the shade and watch the butterflies flitting from flower to flower.

But all too soon the hours slipped by, and it was time to pack up the picnic baskets and return home. It had been a truly delightful day.

The day of scrapes

The following week, Katy had a *dreadful* day. Nothing seemed to go right for her.

First of all, she was late for school because the ribbon had come off her bonnet. She had tried to pin it in place, but Aunt Izzie had insisted on sewing it back on. By the time Katy and Clover arrived at Miss Knight's School for Girls, they were late for the first lesson.

'It's all Aunt Izzie's fault,' muttered Katy. Miss Knight gave her a black mark for being late, and another one for her untidy writing. When the bell rang for playtime, Katy couldn't wait to run outside.

Next to the playground was another girls' school – Miss Miller's. The Knight girls and the Miller girls were sworn enemies. Katy sat up on the woodshed roof. She could see into the Miller playground from there.

Suddenly a gust of wind lifted Katy's bonnet (which she hadn't bothered to tie on properly) and carried it over the fence. Katy stared in horror as her bonnet landed in the middle of the Miller school playground.

At any minute the Miller girls would appear. Katy could imagine the fun they would have with her bonnet, dancing around it, waving it in the air, even using it as a football! Quickly, Katy jumped down from the woodshed and climbed over the fence. She ran across the playground, snatched the bonnet, then raced back to the fence. She scrambled back just as the Miller girls poured into the playground. Her friends crowded round her, cheering and patting her on the back.

After so much excitement, the rest of the morning seemed very dull. So, as soon as Miss Knight had gone home for her lunch, Katy invented a game to play in the classroom.

Each girl was a river, and Katy was Father Ocean. The rivers ran up and down between the rows of desks. Father Ocean leapt up and down on Miss Knight's platform, roaring loudly. Every now and then, Katy would shout, 'Now for a meeting of the waters!' Then all the rivers would turn and run, scrambling and screaming, towards the ocean.

The girls had a marvellous time, rushing up and down, screaming at the tops of their voices. But what a dreadful noise they were making! Even people going past in the street stopped to ask what was going on.

When Miss Knight returned she was startled to see that a crowd had gathered outside the school. She hurried up the steps and threw open the door. The classroom was in an uproar, with chairs overturned, desks pushed to one side and ink spilled on the floor. There were books scattered everywhere.

When the rivers saw Miss Knight they came to a sudden halt. Only Father Ocean still roared and leapt about on the platform.

'What is the meaning of this?' demanded Miss Knight.

At the sound of her voice, Katy froze. Her heart gave a thump. 'It was my idea to play this game,' she admitted in a small voice.

Miss Knight was furious. The girls felt terribly ashamed, especially Katy. Miss Knight had some very stern words to say to all of them. Then she stood over the girls while they cleared up the mess they had made.

That night, Katy told Papa all about her dreadful day. 'Papa,' she asked, 'why is it that on some days *everything* seems to go wrong? If Aunt Izzie hadn't made me late for school, I'm sure I wouldn't have got into so many scrapes.'

Papa asked what Aunt Izzie had done to make Katy late. Katy told him about her bonnet ribbon.

'So, Katy my dear,' he said, smiling, 'if you had mended the ribbon yourself, last night, none of this would have happened. Don't you know the old saying, "For the want of a nail"?'

Katy hadn't heard it before, so Papa told her:

'For the want of a nail the shoe was lost,
For the want of a shoe the horse was lost,
For the want of a horse the rider was lost,
For the want of a rider the battle was lost,
For the want of a battle the kingdom was lost,
And all for the want of a horseshoe nail.'

'Oh, Papa,' exclaimed Katy, 'I shall never, *ever*, forget that!'

But it wasn't long before Katy *did* forget.

Kikeri

A week later, Katy was in disgrace again.

Aunt Izzie had gone out for the evening. Papa was also out, visiting patients, so Katy was in charge. Aunt Izzie had told her to be sure that the children were all in bed by nine o'clock.

At first, everything went smoothly. After supper Katy got Phil ready for bed. He was soon tucked up and fast asleep.

But then the children decided to play *Kikeri*.
Kikeri was a sort of hide-and-seek in the dark.
Aunt Izzie had forbidden the children to play this
particular game. But Papa had never said they
mustn't play it, and Katy always paid more
attention to Papa than to Aunt Izzie.

It wasn't long before the game became more
and more boisterous. Chairs and tables were
knocked over as the children stumbled about in
the darkness. Then Clover thought it would be a
splendid idea to hide on the mantelpiece. When
Katy caught hold of a foot she couldn't imagine
where it had come from.

Of course, the children were enjoying
themselves too much to notice the mess they

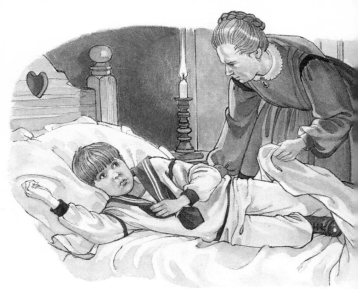

were making. Then suddenly, above all the noise in the nursery, Katy heard the sound of the carriage door slamming.

Aunt Izzie! To her horror, Katy realised that it was ten o'clock. At once, the children fled to their bedrooms.

Aunt Izzie came quietly upstairs. Dorry and John were snoring rather noisily, she thought. And their beds looked strangely lumpy. She pulled back the bedspreads. Both children were fully clothed! They even had their shoes on!

Aunt Izzie looked ready to explode. She made Dorry and John undress while she stood over them like an angry dragon. Then she tucked them into bed.

Elsie was lying on top of her bed. She was still dressed, too, but no amount of shaking would wake her.

Aunt Izzie stormed into the room shared by Katy and Clover. They were both in tears as Aunt Izzie scolded them.

The next morning Katy wept even more when Papa spoke very seriously to her. He reminded her of the time when Mama died. She had said, 'Katy must be a Mama to the little ones when she grows up.'

Papa said he thought the time had come. Katy was old enough now to look after her brothers and sisters. As for Kikeri, it was never played again.

Cousin Helen

The long summer holiday had just begun, when the Carr family had some exciting news.

'Cousin Helen is coming to stay for a few days,' announced Aunt Izzie.

Cousin Helen! The children had often been told about her, but they had never met her. She was an invalid. She couldn't walk, but had to lie on a sofa, day after day. Papa visited her twice a year, and often talked about her.

'She is such a good, kind person,' he said. 'Although she is often in great pain, she never complains or grumbles. She thinks only of other people all the time. You should all try to be like her,' he added, looking at Katy in particular.

When Helen's carriage arrived, the children felt a little shy. But Helen called them to her in a bright, cheery, voice and gave them all warm hugs and kisses. Soon they were the best of friends.

Once Helen was settled in the guest room, the children were allowed to go up and see her. Katy noticed at once that the room looked different. Somehow it seemed prettier than before. Aunt Izzie always kept the house clean and tidy, but it was never *pretty*.

Katy admired a lovely white vase on the mantelpiece. It was Helen's favourite ornament. She took it with her everywhere. Katy ran outside to pick the loveliest flowers in the garden. She gave them to Helen, who arranged them in the white vase.

The children spent many happy hours in Helen's room. She was so good at story telling, and she knew all sorts of games. Even Aunt Izzie and Papa joined in the fun.

The children grew to love Helen. Katy liked nothing more than to sit with her, once her brothers and sisters had gone to bed. They talked and talked about all sorts of things.

All too soon it was time for Helen to leave.
She was going away for a holiday. Before she
went, she gave everyone a farewell present.
There were toys and books for the younger
children, a notebook for Papa and a brooch for
Aunt Izzie. As for Katy, she gasped with delight
when Helen gave her a white vase exactly like
her own. 'I shall keep it for ever!' she cried.

'If you do, it will be the first thing you've ever
kept for more than a week without breaking it,'
remarked Aunt Izzie.

As she waved goodbye to Helen, Katy had to
brush away the tears from her eyes. 'I *will* try to
be good like Helen,' she thought, 'and I shall
start tomorrow.'

Tomorrow

But when tomorrow came, Katy didn't feel like being good. As she was brushing her hair, her elbow knocked against the precious white vase. It fell to the floor and broke into a hundred pieces. Katy burst into tears.

'You clumsy child!' cried Aunt Izzie. 'And fancy crying like a baby, at your age,' she added crossly. Then she told Katy to tidy her drawer before going downstairs to play.

'And you are not to play on the new swing today,' she continued. The new swing had just been put up in the woodshed, but it wasn't fastened properly at the top. Perhaps Aunt Izzie should have explained this to Katy.

Katy thought Aunt Izzie very unkind to make her stay indoors on such a lovely morning. But she tidied her drawer as she had been told. Then she raced downstairs.

Elsie was just coming up to see Katy. 'Look,' she said, 'I've written a letter to Helen. Now I'm going to post it.' This made Katy even more upset. *She* wanted to be the first to write to Helen.

'I don't care about your stupid letter,' she said, giving Elsie an impatient push. Elsie slipped, screamed, and fell down the stairs.

Aunt Izzie came running into the hall. 'Katy pushed me,' sobbed Elsie. 'She's a naughty, wicked girl!'

'Well, Katy Carr,' cried Aunt Izzie, 'you should be ashamed of yourself. What would Helen think of you?'

The thought of Helen made Katy even more miserable. She ran outside, so that Aunt Izzie shouldn't see the tears that were welling up in her eyes.

25

The swing

As she passed the woodshed, Katy caught sight of the new swing. Trust Aunt Izzie to spoil her fun! Why *shouldn't* she play on the new swing today?

So Katy sat on the smooth wooden seat. Holding the thick new ropes, she pushed gently with her toes. The swing lifted her up into the air and she swung backwards and forwards. It was a wonderful feeling. Her hair fanned out in the breeze. She felt peaceful and dreamy. The swing lifted her higher and higher.

All of a sudden, the swing gave a violent twist. It spun round, tossing Katy into the air. She tried to clutch the rope, but felt herself falling down, down, down. Then everything went black.

When at last she opened her eyes, Katy was lying on the sofa in the dining room. Clover was kneeling beside her. She looked pale and frightened. Aunt Izzie was pressing something cold and wet on Katy's forehead.

'What happened?' gasped Katy in a faint voice. Her throat felt very dry.

'Oh, she's alive! She's alive!' sobbed Clover, throwing her arms around Katy's neck.

'Hush, dear,' said Aunt Izzie. Her voice sounded unusually gentle. 'You've had a bad tumble, Katy. Do you remember the swing?'

'Oh yes – the swing,' Katy repeated. 'Did I fall off the new swing?'

'It wasn't fastened properly,' said Aunt Izzie. 'Did you forget that I told you not to play on it today?'

'No, Aunt Izzie. I didn't forget. I...' But Katy couldn't say any more. She closed her eyes. Tears rolled from under the lids.

'Please don't cry,' whispered Clover. 'Aunt Izzie won't scold you.' But Katy was too weak and shaken *not* to cry. She tried to sit up, but found she couldn't move.

When Dr Carr came home he was shocked to see Katy looking so ill. He felt her legs and her back. Then he and Aunt Izzie carried her gently and carefully upstairs.

Poor Katy. The pain in her back was dreadful. She lay in bed, unable to move. She was very hot and *so* uncomfortable. She had meant to go to Paradise that afternoon, with Clover. If only she hadn't gone on the swing! If only... but then Katy must have fallen asleep.

When she next opened her eyes she could feel a lovely cool breeze. Elsie was sitting by the bed, waving a palm-leaf fan. Katy started to say something, but began to cry instead.

'Poor Katy,' whispered Elsie. 'Is it terribly sore?'

'It isn't that,' sobbed Katy. 'I've been so horrid to you. Please forgive me for pushing you.'

At once, Elsie hugged Katy and the two sisters kissed each other.

Later that day Papa brought another doctor to see Katy. The doctor spent a long time examining her. When at last he had finished he told Katy that she would have to stay in bed for at least a week, possibly longer.

Papa looked very worried. He bent over Katy and kissed her hot forehead. 'You must learn to be patient, my darling,' he said quietly. Katy couldn't reply. She just lay there, trying to hold back the tears.

The nightmare

Katy lay in bed, counting the days to the end of the week. But when at last seven days had gone by, she was no better. When she tried to sit up it hurt so much that she was glad to sink back against the soft pillows.

Then, instead of getting better, the pain became a great deal worse. Katy didn't know it at the time, but she was very ill indeed. Aunt Izzie was often up most of the night looking after her. The other children tiptoed around the house. There were times when Katy didn't know whether it was day or night. Or even whether she was asleep or awake.

Then one day, the pain did not seem so bad. Katy opened her eyes. Was the nightmare over

at last? 'How long have I been ill?' she asked Papa, who was at her bedside.

'It's four weeks since your fall,' he replied.

'As long as that? And when can I get up and go downstairs again?' she asked.

Her father looked very grave. 'Your back will take a long time to get better, I'm afraid,' he said. 'But you are young and strong and it *will* get better. Think of poor Helen. You must be brave, as she is. She will never walk again.'

Katy buried her face in Papa's chest. 'Oh Papa, Papa,' she sobbed. 'If only I had listened to Aunt Izzie! I wish I could be brave like Helen.'

Then she wept as if her heart would break.

Dismal days

Now that Katy knew she wasn't going to get better for a long, long time, she felt thoroughly miserable. The family tried to cheer her up, but Katy's unhappiness made her selfish and thoughtless. Aunt Izzie ran up and downstairs all day, and was always trying to please her. But Katy never said, 'Thank you.' And she never noticed how tired Aunt Izzie looked.

She didn't even want Cecy or her sisters and brothers to come and see her. It only made her feel worse to hear about all the fun they were having downstairs, or outside in the sunshine. She refused to let the sun into her room. It only made her feel more miserable. So she lay alone in her gloomy bedroom, not speaking to anyone and not wanting to do anything.

But the nights were worse. Once everyone else was asleep, Katy would lie awake, crying helplessly, for hours on end. All her plans would run through her head — all the beautiful things she wanted to do when she was grown up. 'And now I shall never do anything at all, except lie here,' she would say to herself. 'Papa says I shall get better. But I know I won't. It's so *awful*.' Then she would weep and weep until morning. No wonder she was so short-tempered every day!

One morning a letter arrived from Helen. She was on her way home from her holiday, but didn't think she should stay with the Carrs this time. Aunt Izzie would be too busy looking after Katy.

When Katy heard this, she begged Papa and Aunt Izzie to invite Helen to stay, if only for one night. Papa said it would mean too much work for Aunt Izzie.

But Aunt Izzie knew how happy Katy would be to see her cousin, so she said, 'Yes.' For the first time in her life, Katy threw her arms around Aunt Izzie's neck and kissed her.

Cousin Helen to the rescue

When Helen arrived, she was shocked to see Katy's sad, pale face. Katy's eyes were red and swollen from so much crying, and she had become quite thin. But oh, how happy she was to see her cousin!

They kissed, and talked for a little while. Then Helen asked if the blinds could be pulled up. 'It's so dark and dismal in here,' she said. 'Does the sunlight hurt your eyes, my dear?'

Katy replied that she hated to see the sun. It only reminded her of the lovely times she used to have.

Helen thought hard for a minute. Then she turned to Katy. 'Listen to me, Katy,' she said in a serious voice. 'You are going to get better one day. You know that, don't you?'

'Yes,' replied Katy, 'but it's going to be such a long time to wait. And I wanted to do so many things. Now I can't do any of them.'

'What sort of things did you want to do?' asked Helen. Katy told her that she had wanted to be famous and to be loved and admired by everyone. And she had promised Mama to take care of her brothers and sisters.

Helen told her that there were plenty of things she could still do. First of all, her sickroom should be a bright, pretty place, full of sunshine and fresh flowers. The old medicine bottles which cluttered up the mantelpiece should be put away.

Then Helen brushed Katy's tangled hair, and promised to send her a pretty dressing gown instead of the rather plain one she was wearing. 'Each day you must think, ''Soon I will be better. But in the meantime I must make my sickroom pretty so that everyone will want to share it with me.'' Then you must always be ready to welcome your sisters and brothers when they come to see you. Be interested in what everyone else is doing or thinking. Then they will come to you whenever they want to talk or to ask advice.'

Helen also made Katy promise to do two hours' school work each day, so that she wouldn't fall so far behind the others. When Papa came to take Helen to her room, Katy promised to remember everything Helen had told her.

That night she slept peacefully for the first time since her fall.

Christmas

Two long months passed. Katy still had to lie
in bed all the time. But she tried to look forward
to each new day, and to be happy for her
family's sake. Her room was always cheerful
and cosy, even on a cold winter's day. Outside,
the snow was falling, but in Katy's room a fire
burned brightly in the grate.

Soon it would be Christmas. It was decided
that the children should hang up their stockings
in Katy's room. Then she wouldn't miss any of
the fun.

Katy had made a list of the presents she
wanted to give to the family. But she couldn't
go to the shops, and she didn't have enough
money. So she asked Aunt Izzie for help. To her
delight, Aunt Izzie gave her a five dollar note.
'This is your Christmas present,' she explained,
'but perhaps you would like it now.'

'How good you are!' exclaimed Katy, beaming with pleasure. Aunt Izzie was always so kind and gentle these days.

Katy gave Aunt Izzie her list and the money. The next day Aunt Izzie returned from town laden with parcels. Katy spent a happy afternoon wrapping everything up.

On Christmas Eve the children hung up their stockings. Katy couldn't help wishing that someone would pin up a stocking for *her*. Later, Katy helped Papa and Aunt Izzie to fill the

stockings. The toes were stuffed with candy and oranges. Then came the parcels, all shapes and sizes, wrapped in white paper and tied with brightly coloured ribbon.

The next morning, Phil was at Katy's bedside, shaking her awake. 'Merry Christmas!' he cried. 'Look what Santa Claus has brought!'

Katy rubbed her eyes and gasped with delight.
Next to her bed was the most beautiful little
Christmas tree she had ever seen. Its branches
were hung with oranges
and shiny red apples.
There were baskets of
nuts and strings of
bright berries, and
small parcels tied with
satin ribbon.
'What a beautiful
Christmas tree!'
exclaimed Katy.

'We all helped
to decorate it,'
explained Clover.
'But haven't you
noticed what it's
standing on?'

39

Katy looked. She saw a rather curious chair. It had a long cushioned back and a footstool attached at the front. This was Papa's present to Katy. Soon she would be well enough to sit in it.

It was a wonderful Christmas. The children declared it to be the best ever. Katy couldn't quite agree with them, but she had certainly enjoyed herself.

A new lesson to learn

It was several weeks before Katy was well enough to use the new chair. Aunt Izzie would dress her in the morning and slide her off the bed onto the chair. Then she would wheel her over to the window. Every movement was painful, but it was marvellous to be able to sit up and

look outside! Katy could see the sky and the trees, and watch the people go by in the street. With each day she grew brighter and more cheerful.

So the weeks and months slipped by. When summer came the days were long and hot. The heat made Katy feel very uncomfortable. How she longed to run into the cool shade under the poplar trees. It was now a whole year since her fall. Would she *ever* be well again?

One day Papa took her for a drive, thinking that she would enjoy going out for a change. But the ride was so bumpy, and it was so painful being lifted in and out of the carriage, that she couldn't bear to do it again.

At last September came. It brought a fresh breeze, smelling of pine woods and cool hilltops. Katy began to feel much better. She even asked Papa if she could have French lessons. So the French teacher came to her room twice a week. Katy worked very hard, and became one of his best pupils. She always tried to be cheerful, but she dreaded the dismal winter days that lay ahead.

Then something happened that was to change her life. Aunt Izzie had not been feeling well. Papa said that she must stay in bed for a few days. It seemed strange not to see her bustling about the house, in charge of everything. Katy missed her dreadfully. She was so used to having her there whenever she needed anything.

One day Papa looked very worried. He told Katy that Aunt Izzie had a serious illness called typhoid fever. She needed plenty of rest, and peace and quiet.

It was an anxious time for the family. The children couldn't wait for Aunt Izzie to get better. It never occurred to them that she might *not* get better.

Then one morning Katy woke to find Mary, the maid, at her bedside. Mary was crying quietly. Aunt Izzie had died in the night. The children wept in one another's arms. What would they do without Aunt Izzie to look after them?

For the next few weeks the house was sad and gloomy. Papa said they would have to find a housekeeper. But Katy hated the thought of a stranger coming to live with them. 'I shall be housekeeper!' she cried. 'I can organise everything from my bedroom. Oh please say yes, Papa. It would give me something really important to do.' Papa didn't think that Katy would be able to manage. But he agreed to let her try.

At first, Katy was always worrying that the children weren't eating properly, or that the house wasn't clean enough. But after a few ups and downs, Papa saw that things seemed to be running smoothly. So Katy remained in charge of the household from that day on.

At last...

Time passed, and it was now two years since Aunt Izzie had died. Katy was just like a mother to her sisters and brothers. Her room was everyone's favourite place, full of fresh flowers and pretty things.

Although she still couldn't walk, Katy didn't have to sit in her chair all day. Instead, she had a wheelchair. She could move around her room and fetch things without always having to ask for help.

Clover was growing up, too. She was quite a young lady now. Her thick brown hair was pinned up, instead of hanging in two plaits. And her dresses, like Katy's, were always neat and tidy.

45

Then, one day, Elsie and Clover were startled to hear Katy crying out. She sounded very excited about something, so they rushed up to her room at once. To their astonishment they found Katy standing up, holding onto her wheelchair!

'Look at me!' cried Katy. 'I suddenly felt that I *could* stand up, if I really tried. And I can!'

'Papa, Papa!' shrieked Clover. 'Come and see Katy! Dorry, John, Phil — come quickly!'

The rest of the family crowded into the room. Papa could hardly believe his eyes. 'This is marvellous, my dear!' he cried. 'But you must be careful not to overdo things. Sit down now, and have a rest.' He helped Katy to sit back in her wheelchair.

'Oh, Papa,' she gasped, her voice trembling with excitement. 'Shall I be able to walk again, soon?'

'Yes, my dear,' replied Papa, 'I'm sure that you will soon be completely better. But it may take a little longer. You must be patient.'

The next day, Katy stood up again. And this time she took a step forward! Elsie and Clover kept close to her in case she should fall.

In the weeks that followed, Katy's legs became stronger and stronger. Soon she could take several steps at once, pushing a chair along in front of her.

At last she was able to move without leaning on the chair. For the first time in four long years she walked out of her bedroom. How marvellous it felt. She noticed all the changes that had taken place — a new bookshelf in Phil's room, some pretty curtains in Elsie's room. Everywhere seemed fresh and new.

'Can I go downstairs now, Papa?' she asked one day. 'I'm sure my legs are strong enough.'

But Papa said she must wait a little longer. Then Clover had an idea. 'Why don't we have a family celebration on the day Katy comes downstairs?'

Everyone thought it was a splendid idea. Papa said Katy should be well enough to go downstairs in ten days' time.

Clover seemed to be very busy during the following week or so. She wanted the whole house to be spick-and-span for the big day. The younger children seemed to be sharing a secret. Katy could see that Phil was almost bursting with excitement about something. But she didn't want to spoil the fun, so she didn't ask any questions.

On the day before the celebration, Clover asked Katy to keep her bedroom door closed. 'We have to sweep the hall,' she explained, 'and you don't want dust in your room, do you?'

Katy's big day dawned at last. She put on a pretty new dress. It was a present from Papa. Her sisters had new dresses, too.

'How nice we all look!' cried Elsie.

Papa took Katy's arm. Very slowly they made their way downstairs. 'Let's go into the parlour,' said Papa. 'You need to rest now, my dear.'

Papa opened the parlour door. Katy took one step forward – then stopped. She held onto the doorknob. Her face was flushed. For one awful moment Papa thought she was going to faint. Then she took a step forward and almost *ran* across the room.

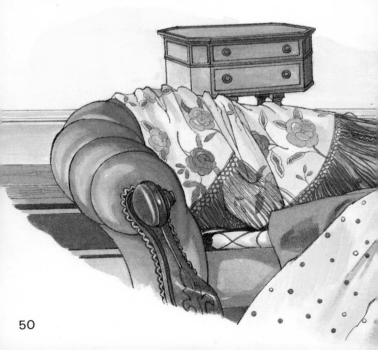

'Cousin Helen!' she gasped. She almost threw herself down by the sofa where her cousin lay. The two hugged each other, laughing and crying at the same time.

'Wasn't it a nice surprise!' cried Phil, jumping up and down in great excitement.

Katy had never felt so happy. How lucky she was to have such a wonderful family! This was the best day of her life. As long as she lived, she would never forget it.

More
WRINKLIES'
WIT & WISDOM

First published in 2006 by

Sevenoaks
an imprint of the
Carlton Publishing Group
20 Mortimer Street
London W1T 3JW

2 4 6 8 10 9 7 5 3 1

A catalogue record for this book is available from the British Library

ISBN-13: 978-1-86200-331-6
ISBN-10: 1-86200-331-9

Typeset by E-Type
Printed in Great Britain
by Mackays

More WRINKLIES' WIT & WISDOM

Humorous Quotes
About Getting on a Bit

Compiled by Allison Vale & Alison Rattle

SEVENOAKS

Contents

Introduction

The human race is unique in its enlistment of grandparents into the work of rearing the young. Studies among indigenous tribes have proven that the presence of a grandmother within the family unit will greatly improve the survival rates of any children. This gives the human race an advantage over all other species, for improved survival rates lead to greater longevity, which in turn leads to more grandparents and so on and so on.

This means that we have the audacious luck to live for twice as long as our nearest relative, the chimpanzee. The poor old female chimp expires shortly after she loses her fertility, while the human female could enjoy up to 50 years plus following the end of her fertile years. What a bonus!

Life for the over 50s has never been better. Women can now expect to live well into their 80s with men following close on their heels. This has given birth to an anti-ageing fad which takes full advantage of this spectacular longevity. The cross-over from adulthood into old age is becoming progressively blurred. With the growing popularity and acceptability of cosmetic surgery, many people now choose to deny the ageing process altogether (some with more success than others: Sharon Osbourne looks sensational, not so Jackie Stallone).

We must not forget that the autumn years serve their own purpose and should be embraced. There is an African proverb that illustrates beautifully how other cultures elevate age: 'The death of an old person is like the loss of a library.' Western societies are losing sight of this like never before. From both sides of the Atlantic we risk being overwhelmed by the new cult of celebrity. It is an inexhaustible quarry: periodically, someone sees fit to carve out another vacuous wannabe, bursting with youth, sex appeal and a psychotic need for fame. Often, talent is an irrelevance. Anyone willing to play strip poker live on national TV, eat unimaginable grubs in an Australian jungle, or disgrace themselves on a TV talent show, can grab their fleeting 15 minutes. Comedy baby naming is even turning the offspring of celebrities into readymade mini-celebrities. It's so dreary.

In truth, growing old is not what it used to be. Thanks to huge advances in medical science and the propensity of the media to bombard us with sleek visions of ageless, airbrushed celebrities, breaking the age barrier is easier than ever. Whoever now thinks of 50 or even 60 as being particularly old? Mick Jagger with his pants pulled over his belly; Joan Collins in wrinkled support tights? Not likely! Our healthier lifestyles and the invention of lycra undergarments have driven the physical signs of ageing back at least a decade. Look around any pub, theatre or nightclub, and you'll be sure to see plenty of vintage verve. The silver set are out there grabbing life by the throat as much, if not more, than the younger generation.

So, it is time we stop dishing out lifetime achievement awards that pay quiet lip service to 50-plus talents as we brush them aside. The names in this collection have energy, vibrancy and longevity. Retirement, for many of them, is out of the question.

This compilation celebrates the geniuses and giants of our time. The kind of professional entertainers who can still pull together three generations of a family around the TV and guarantee that everyone's laughing. The heavyweight actors

Introduction

who have put in decades of graft and now lend an emotional depth and gravitas to any scene. We challenge the stereotypes that this cult of celebrity would have us adopt: many here are sexy, sassy and sophisticated seniors who are still smouldering on screen and can give any skimpily clad 'artiste' something to wail about. Laugh along with Woody Allen, John Cleese, Julie Walters, Whoopi Goldberg and more, as they observe life's joys, trials and irritations.

The wrinkly years are not to be denied, reviled or feared, but to be welcomed and enjoyed. Forget a quiet, dignified old age and party on!

Growing Old is...

...when 'getting lucky' means finding your car in the car park.

...when an 'all nighter' means not getting up to pee.

...when 'getting a little action' means you don't need to eat any fibre.

...when you're told to slow down by the doctor instead of the police.

...when going bra-less pulls all the wrinkles out of your face.

...when a sexy babe catches your attention and your pacemaker opens the garage door.

...when your friends compliment you on your new alligator shoes and you're barefoot.

...when your wife says, 'Let's go upstairs and make love,' and you answer, 'Honey, I can't do both!'

...when you remember when it cost more to run a car than to park it.

All Anonymous

…when you've met so many people that every new person you meet reminds you of someone else.

Ogden Nash

Youthful Thinking

I never felt that there was anything enviable in youth. I cannot recall that any of us, as youths, admired our condition to excess or had a desire to prolong it.

Bernard Berenson

Zeal, n. A certain nervous disorder afflicting the young and inexperienced.

Ambrose Bierce

Youth would be an ideal state if it came a little later in life.

Herbert Asquith

Youth is a wonderful thing. What a crime to waste it on children.

George Bernard Shaw

American youth attributes much more importance to arriving at driver's licence age than at voting age.

Marshall McLuhan

When we are young we are slavishly employed in procuring something whereby we may live comfortably when we grow old; and when we are old, we perceive it is too late to live as we proposed.

Alexander Pope

It is better to waste one's youth than to do nothing with it at all.

Georges Courteline

I'm aiming by the time I'm 50 to stop being an adolescent.

Wendy Cope

I live in that solitude which is painful in youth, but delicious in the years of maturity.

Albert Einstein

Youth is like spring, an overpraised season.

Samuel Butler

Old age at least gives me an excuse for not being very good at things that I was not very good at when I was young.

Thomas Sowell

We are only young once. That is all society can stand.

Bob Bowen

When you are young, you want to be the master of your fate and the captain of your soul. When you are older, you will settle for being the master of your weight and the captain of your bowling team.

Anon

In youth we run into difficulties. In old age difficulties run into us.

Beverly Sills

You're only as old as you feel… but you can't be Shirley Temple on the Good Ship Lollipop forever. Sooner or later, damnit, you're old.

Joan Crawford

If youth knew; if age could.

Henri Estienne

Till Death Us Do Part

My wife and I were happy for 20 years. Then we met.

Rodney Dangerfield

I married the first man I ever kissed. When I tell this to my children they just about throw up.

Barbara Bush

Some people ask the secret of our long marriage. We take time to go to a restaurant two times a week. A little candlelight, dinner, soft music and dancing. She goes Tuesdays, I go Fridays.

Henny Youngman

My wife and I tried to breakfast together, but we had to stop or our marriage would have been wrecked.

Winston Churchill

In mid-life the man wants to see how irresistible he still is to younger women. How they turn their hearts to stone and more or less commit a murder of their marriage I just don't know, but they do.

Patricia Neal

When asked his secret of love, being married 54 years to the same person, he said, 'Ruth and I are happily incompatible.'

Billy Graham

I've been in love with the same woman for 49 years. If my wife ever finds out, she'll kill me.

Henny Youngman

Ann Meara of the comedy team Stiller and Meara observed a while ago in a *New York Times* interview of her 30-plus year-marriage, 'Was it love at first sight? It wasn't then – but it sure is now.'

Ann Meara

Till Death Us Do Part

You, that are going to be married, think things can never be done too fast: but we that are old, and know what we are about, must elope methodically, madam.

Oliver Goldsmith

No man or woman really knows what perfect love is until they have been married a quarter of a century.

Mark Twain

My new wife is 32 and I'm 70. She's rejuvenated me totally. It's so exciting to see life through the eyes of a modern girl.

Wilbur Smith

Sheila and I just celebrated our thirtieth wedding anniversary. Somebody asked her, what was our secret? She answered, 'On my wedding day, I decided to make a list of 10 of Tim's faults which, for the sake of our marriage, I would always overlook. I figured I could live with at least 10!' When she was asked which faults she had listed, Sheila replied, 'I never did get around to listing them. Instead, every time he does something that makes me mad, I simply say to myself, "Lucky for him, it's one of the 10!"'

Tim Hudson, Chicken Soup for the Romantic Soul

There is no greater happiness for a man than approaching a door at the end of a day knowing someone on the other side of that door is waiting for the sound of his footsteps.

Ronald Reagan

The other night I said to my wife Ruth, 'Do you feel that the sex and excitement have gone out of our marriage?' She said, 'I'll discuss it with you during the next commercial.'

Milton Berle

One Christmas my husband gave me a chenille hand–knitted bobble hat. It was like we'd never met. I opened it and I said, 'Did you not like me when you bought me this?'

Arabella Weir

I'd marry again if I found a man who had 15 million dollars, would sign over half to me, and guarantee that he'd be dead within a year.

Bette Davis

I've had an exciting time. I married for love and got a little money along with it.

Rose Fitzgerald Kennedy

We were just happy to be in the same room together.

Judi Dench, on her long marriage to Michael Williams

Till Death Us Do Part

Before marriage, a man will lie awake all night thinking about something you've said. After marriage, he'll fall asleep before you finish saying it.

Helen Rowland

I suppose when they reach a certain age some men are afraid to grow up. It seems the older the men get, the younger their new wives get.

Elizabeth Taylor

As you get older, you realise it's work. It's that fine line between love and companionship. But passionate love? I'd love to know how to make that last.

Tracey Ullman

All marriages are happy. It's trying to live together afterwards that causes all the problems.

Shelley Winters

Instead of getting married again, I'm going to find a woman I don't like and just give her a house.

Rod Stewart

The man or woman you really love will never grow old to you. Through the wrinkles of time, through the bowed frame of years, you will always see the dear face and feel the warm heart union of your eternal love.

Alfred A. Montapert

My husband, like most men, can only do one thing at a time. If there's two cups of tea to be made, they'll make one. And then they'll make another one after that. If my husband's going to the shop and I say, 'Can you get a loaf of bread and a pint of milk?' he'll come back with one or the other. Never both.

Linda Robson, Grumpy Old Women

Before marriage, a man will lay down his life for you; after marriage he won't even lay down his newspaper.

Helen Rowland

Marriage is like a cage; one sees the birds outside desperate to get in, and those inside desperate to get out.

Ogden Nash

The conception of two people living together for 25 years without having a cross word suggests a lack of spirit only to be admired in sheep.

Alan Patrick Herbert

Till Death Us Do Part

My wife Mary and I have been married for 47 years and not once have we had an argument serious enough to consider divorce; murder, yes, but divorce, never.

Jack Benny

Men have got no reason to be grumpy at all [at Christmas time], because they don't have to do anything. They really don't do anything. In fact, my husband goes out on Christmas Eve to buy my present. He's had 364 days to go and get it, and he goes on Christmas Eve.

Linda Robson, Grumpy Old Women

I never knew what real happiness was until I got married, and by then it was too late.

Max Kaufman

Bigamy is having one wife too many. Marriage is the same.

Oscar Wilde

That married couples can live together day after day is a miracle that the Vatican has overlooked.

Bill Cosby

After about 20 years of marriage, I'm finally starting to scratch the surface of that one. And I think the answer lies somewhere between conversation and chocolate.

Mel Gibson, when asked if he knew what women want

We do not squabble, fight or have rows. We collect grudges. We're in an arms race, storing up warheads for the domestic Armageddon.

Hugh Leonard

On my sixtieth birthday my wife gave me a superb birthday present. She let me win an argument.

Anon

Basically my wife was immature. I'd be at home in the bath and she'd come in and sink my boats.

Woody Allen

Women! I have no idea. I don't know anything about women at all. They're a complete mystery to me.

Bryan Ferry

I was married for 30 years. Isn't that enough? I've had my share of dirty underwear on the floor.

Martha Stewart

Your marriage is in trouble if your wife says, 'You're only interested in one thing,' and you can't remember what it is.

Milton Berle

There's one thing about a late marriage – it doesn't last long.

Elderly Irishman, talking on Irish TV
about courting in the 1940s

A friend recently told us about a 25th anniversary party where the husband gave a toast and said, 'The key to our success is very simple. Within minutes after every fight, one of us says, "I'm sorry, Sally".'

Cokie and Steve Roberts

I haven't spoken to my wife in years. I didn't want to interrupt her.

Rodney Dangerfield

We are so fond of one another, because our ailments are the same.

Jonathan Swift

To see a young couple loving each other is no wonder, but to see an old couple loving each other is the best sight of all.

William Makepeace Thackeray

I swear there are drugs in the upholstery of his chair. Because honestly he just gets near the television and goes zzz… It's known as the drugged chair.

Dillie Keane, Grumpy Old Women

Sexy at Sixty

I know nothing about sex because I was always married.

Zsa Zsa Gabor

Before we make love my husband takes a pain killer.

Joan Rivers

The Three Ages of Marriage: 20 is when you watch the TV after. 40 is when you watch the TV during. 60 is when you watch the TV instead.

Anon

After a man passes 60, his mischief is mainly in his head.

Washington Irving

Men of my age are just too old, and the younger ones may have the energy but they don't have the intellect.

Cilla Black

You know you're getting older when you have sex with someone half your age and it's legal.

Dan Savage

Statistics show that at the age of 70, there are five women to every man. Isn't that the darnedest time for a guy to get those odds?

Anon

The longer thread of life we spin
The more occasion still to sin.

Robert Herrick

Sexy at Sixty

When a girl's under 21 she's protected by the law.
When she is over 65, she's protected by nature and
anywhere in between, she's fair game.

Cary Grant

What is a younger woman? I'm pretty old, so
almost every woman is younger than me.

Jack Nicholson

It seems that after the age of 50, I began to age at
the rate of about three years per year. I began
falling asleep 15 minutes into an episode of
Seinfeld. I also began falling asleep during sex rather
than after.

Anon

When they were asked what they thought of a
phone mast being erected on the adjacent military
museum, one 97-year-old raised his hand to ask,
'Will it make us sterile?'

General Sir Jeremy MacKenzie, referring to a Chelsea
pensioner

You still chase women, but only downhill.

Bob Hope, on turning 70

We look forward to a disorderly, vigorous, un-
honoured and disreputable old age.

Don Marquis

Old guys of 50-plus love me with a whip in my hand.

Anne Robinson

Every man over 40 is a scoundrel.

George Bernard Shaw

As you get older, you don't get as horny – I don't take as many cold showers a day as I used to.

Tom Jones

There will be sex after death, we just won't be able to feel it.

Lily Tomlin

You can live without sex but not without glasses.

Anon

At 70, I find orgasmic sex quite dispensable.

Tennessee Williams

75-year-old (celebrating his birthday in a brothel): I haven't had a woman in longer than I care to say. You know she doesn't have to be beautiful – just patient.

Polly Platt and Louis Malle

The pleasures that once were heaven, look silly at 67.

Noel Coward

Sexy at Sixty

Now that I'm over 60, I'm veering towards respectability.

Shelley Winters

I'm still a terrible flirt. It boosts your ego knowing you still have the ability, but that's as far as it goes. Now we have a silly rule – no hands in jumpers.

Antony Worrall Thompson

If you can't have fun as an ageing sex symbol when you hit 60, I don't know what will become of you.

Raquel Welch

I'm not a raver any more, all good things must come to an end.

Jack Nicholson

You don't get older, you get better.

Shirley Bassey

My wild oats have turned to shredded wheat.

Anon

How exciting! This is the first time I've ever been implicated in a sex case. I don't remember handling her breasts. We were just having lunch.

Antony Worrall Thompson, on being accused of having an affair

Mary Wesley has thick white hair, endless legs and the captivating face that made her such a sexy beauty in her youth. Next year she will be 90, which she finds rather irritating because there is nothing elderly about her.

Lynda Lee-Potter

My love life is terrible. The last time I was inside a woman was when I visited the Statue of Liberty.

Woody Allen

I have so little sex appeal that my gynaecologist calls me 'sir'.

Joan Rivers

Clinton lied. A man might forget where he parks or where he lives, but he never forgets oral sex, no matter how bad it is.

Barbara Bush

I'm a different guy here in my 60s. I don't have the same libido. It used to be that I didn't think I could go to sleep if I wasn't involved in some kind of amorous contact. Well, I spend a lot of time sleeping alone these days.

Jack Nicholson

In my next life I'm going to come back as a rather good-looking, even quite fat and plain 50-year-old man, who's just been widowed or sadly divorced, and I would go to the country and I would clean up. I would get a bonk every night of the week.

Jilly Cooper, Grumpy Old Women

Sexy at Sixty

Sex appeal is in your heart and head. I'll be sexy no matter how old or how my body changes.

Sonia Braga

One of the best parts of growing older? You can flirt all you like since you've become harmless.

Liz Smith

Getting older is all about high blood pressure, high cholesterol, high anxiety, and low sex drive. At my age, 'safe sex' is not falling out of bed.

Anon

It's been so long since I've had sex I've forgotten who ties up whom.

Joan Rivers

There are a number of mechanical devices which increase sexual arousal, particularly in women. Chief among these is the Mercedes-Benz 380SL convertible.

P.J. O'Rourke

I had wanted for years to get Mrs Thatcher in front of my camera... as she got more powerful she got sort of sexier.

Helmut Newton

In my outrageous 20s, I asked a charming, chatty Englishwoman I'd met in Villefranche when people stopped having sex. 'It's no good asking me, my dear,' she said. 'I'm only 83.'

Anon

I once had a rose named after me and I was very flattered. But I was not pleased to read the description in the catalogue: no good in a bed, but fine up against a wall.

Eleanor Roosevelt

I was with this girl the other night and from the way she was responding to my skilful caresses, you would have sworn that she was conscious from the top of her head to the tag on her toes.

Emo Philips

My grandmother's 90; she's dating a man 93. They never argue: they can't hear each other.

Cathy Ladman

Having sex at my age is still wonderful, really. It just gets more difficult to see with whom you are having it.

Anon

Viva Viagra

I only take Viagra when I am with more than one woman.

Jack Nicholson

Viva Viagra

Sex at the age of 84 is a wonderful experience. Especially the one in the winter.

Milton Berle

There is more money being spent on breast implants and Viagra than on Alzheimer's research. This means that by 2030, there should be a large elderly population with perky boobs and huge erections and absolutely no recollection of what to do with them.

Anon

At my age, I'm envious of a stiff wind.

Rodney Dangerfield

Everything that goes up must come down. But there comes a time when not everything that's down can come up.

George Burns

An elderly gentleman went to the local drugstore and asked the pharmacist for Viagra. The pharmacist said, 'That's no problem. How many do you want?' The man replied, 'Just a few, maybe half a dozen, but can you cut each one into four pieces?' The pharmacist said, 'That's too small a dose. That won't get you through sex.' The gentleman said, 'Oh, that's all right. I'm past 80 years old, and I don't even think about sex any more. I just want it to stick out far enough so I don't pee on my shoes.'

Anon

Look at Catherine Zeta-Jones and Michael Douglas. She's a clever girl, because like me, she knows that an older man has time to love and nurture you.

Celine Dion

Bob Dole revealed he is one of the test subjects for Viagra. He said on Larry King, 'I wish I had bought stock in it.' Only a Republican would think the best part of Viagra is the fact that you could make money off of it.'

Jay Leno

If I marry again at my age, I'll go on honeymoon to Viagra Falls.

George Burns

An elderly man goes to confession and says to the priest, 'Father, I'm 80 years old, married, have four kids and 11 grandchildren. I started taking Viagra and last night I had an affair and made love to two 18-year-old girls. Both of them. Twice.'

The priest said: 'Well, my son, when was the last time you were in confession?'

'Never, Father, I'm Jewish.'

'So then, why are you telling me?'

'Heck! I'm telling everybody!'

Anon

Old Women...

...will never wake you in the middle of the night to ask, 'What are you thinking?' They don't care what you think.

...look good in bright red lipstick, unlike younger women and drag queens.

...have lived long enough to know how to please a man in ways their daughters could never dream of.

...develop a well-honed sixth sense as they age. They instinctively know when you've goofed up.

...are genetically superior: for every spectacular babe of 70 there is a rotund and receding relic in yellow plaid pants flirting ridiculously with the 22-year-old waitress.

All Anonymous

...are best, because they always think they may be doing it for the last time.

Ian Fleming

Whenever I see an old lady slip and fall on a wet sidewalk, my first instinct is to laugh. But then I think, what if I was an ant, and she fell on me. Then it wouldn't seem quite so funny.

Jack Handey

...are like aging strudels – the crust may not be so lovely, but the filling has come at last into its own.

Robert Farrar Capon

Some turn to vinegar, but the best improve with age.

C.E.M. Joad

Time and trouble will tame an advanced woman, but an advanced old woman is uncontrollable by any earthly force.

Dorothy L. Sayers

What's more beautiful than an old lady with white hair, grown wise with age and able to tell lovely stories about her past?

Brigitte Bardot

There are three classes into which all the women past 70 that ever I knew were to be divided: 1. That dear old soul; 2. That old woman; 3. That old witch.

Samuel Taylor Coleridge

If you want a thing done well, get a couple of old broads to do it.

Bette Davis

Old Men...

...have so much more to offer than young guys. They've done all their running and sown all their wild oats.

Celine Dion

...fall asleep in the middle of television programmes for no apparent reason. In the middle of conversations actually, or is that just me? One minute there's an adult person you're engaging with on some vaguely cerebral level, and the next minute there's somebody quietly snoring.

Kathryn Flett, Grumpy Old Women

...can be short and dumpy and getting bald but if [they have] fire, women will like [them].

Mae West

...are only walking hospitals.

Wentworth Dillon

Old People

Old people don't need companionship. They need to be isolated and studied so it can be determined what nutrients they have that might be extracted for our personal use.

Homer Simpson

At the Harvest Festival in church the area behind the pulpit was piled high with tins of IXL fruit for the old-age pensioners. We had collected the tinned fruit from door to door. Most of it came from old-age pensioners.

Clive James

Old people do more scandalous things than any rebel you want to name. Because they don't give a damn. They couldn't give a rat's ass what you think. They're 80 years old. They're leaving soon, you know what I mean?

Chris Isaak

It would be a good thing if young people were wise, and old people were strong, but God has arranged things better.

Martin Luther

The great secret that all old people share is that you really haven't changed in 70 or 80 years. Your body changes, but you don't change at all. And that, of course, causes great confusion.

Doris Lessing

Generation Gap

One thing only has been lent to youth and age in common – discontent.

Matthew Arnold

Generation Gap

The young do not know enough to be prudent, and therefore they attempt the impossible — and achieve it, generation after generation.

Pearl S. Buck

Young men are apt to think themselves wise enough, as drunken men are apt to think themselves sober enough.

Philip Dormer

My generation, faced as it grew with a choice between religious belief and existential despair, chose marijuana. Now we are in our Cabernet stage.

Peggy Noonan

It's not catastrophes, murders, deaths, diseases, that age and kill us; it's the way people look and laugh, and run up the steps of omnibuses.

Virginia Woolf

It's all that the young can do for the old, to shock them and keep them up to date.

George Bernard Shaw

Actually, I think children should be taught to be bored. I was in a coma of boredom throughout the 70s. The shops weren't even open on a Sunday, and your nanna, both your nannas, came for lunch and you had to be there.

Jenny Eclair, Grumpy Old Women

Methuselah lived to be 969 years old. You boys and girls will see more in the next 50 years than Methuselah saw in his whole lifetime.

Mark Twain

One age blows bubbles and the next breaks them.

William Cowper

But it's hard to be hip over 30 when everyone else is 19, when the last dance we learned was the Lindy, and the last we heard, girls who looked like Barbra Streisand were trying to do something about it.

Judith Viorst

When I was as you are now, towering in the confidence of 21, little did I suspect that I should be at 49, what I now am.

Samuel Johnson

My mother is going to have to stop lying about her age because pretty soon I'm going to be older than she is.

Tripp Evans

The question that is so clearly in many potential parents' minds: 'Why should we stunt our ambitions and impoverish our lives in order to be insulted and looked down upon in our old age?'

Joseph A. Schumpeter

But no matter how they make you feel, you should always watch elders carefully. They were you and you will be them. You carry the seeds of your old age in you at this very moment, and they hear the echoes of their childhood each time they see you.

Kent Nerburn

The main thing wrong with the younger generation is that we aren't in it.

Anon

Sagacity

WISDOM

And in the end, it's not the years in your life that count. It's the life in your years.

Abraham Lincoln

All would live long, but none would be old.

Benjamin Franklin

There are compensations for growing older. One is the realisation that to be sporting isn't at all necessary. It is a great relief to reach this stage of wisdom.

Cornelius Otis Skinner

Despite my 30 years of research into the feminine soul, I have not yet been able to answer the great question that has never been answered: What does a woman want?

Sigmund Freud

No man loves life like him that's growing old.

Sophocles

Old age deprives the intelligent man only of qualities useless to wisdom.

Joseph Joubert

If a human is modest and satisfied, old age will not be heavy on him. If he is not, even youth will be a burden.

Plato

The older I grow, the more I listen to people who don't say much.

Germain G. Glidden

The more sand that has escaped from the hourglass of our life, the clearer we should see through it.

Anon

The man who views the world at 50 the same as he did at 20 has wasted 30 years of his life.

Muhammad Ali

Sagacity

Early to rise and early to bed. Makes a male healthy, wealthy and dead.

James Thurber

If you wait, all that happens is that you get older.

Mario Andretti

Everyone should keep a mental wastepaper basket and the older he grows the more things he will consign to it – torn up to irrecoverable tatters.

Samuel Butler

The thing you realise as you get older is that parents don't know what the hell they're doing and neither will you when you get to be a parent.

Mark Hoppus

As you get older, though, you realise there are fire extinguishers. You do have an ability to control the flames.

Chaka Khan

And you learn as you get older, you learn to play the pauses better.

Michael Parkinson

The older we grow the greater becomes our wonder at how much ignorance one can contain without bursting one's clothes.

Mark Twain

You can tell a lot about a fellow's character by his way of eating jellybeans.

Ronald Reagan

I'm very pleased with each advancing year. It stems back to when I was 40. I was a bit upset about reaching that milestone, but an older friend consoled me. 'Don't complain about growing old – many, many people do not have that privilege.'

Earl Warren

Many are saved from sin by being so inept at it.

Mignon McLaughlin

Life's under no obligation to give us what we expect.

Margaret Mitchell

You can't be brave if you've only had wonderful things happen to you.

Mary Tyler Moore

Wisdom doesn't necessarily come with age. Sometimes age just shows up all by itself.

Tom Wilson

Old age comes at a bad time.

San Banducci

Sagacity

We all take different paths in life, but no matter where we go, we take a little of each other everywhere.

Tim McGraw

Perhaps one has to be very old before one learns to be amused rather than shocked.

Pearl S. Buck

It takes about 10 years to get used to how old you are.

Anon

In three words I can sum up everything I've learned about life: it goes on.

Robert Frost

My father always used to say that when you die, if you've got five real friends, then you've had a great life.

Lee Iacocca

You see things; and you say, 'Why?' But I dream things that never were; and I say, 'Why not?'

George Bernard Shaw

Old age is life's parody.

Simone de Beauvoir

The end comes when we no longer talk with ourselves. It is the end of genuine thinking and the beginning of the final loneliness.

Eric Hoffer

Minds ripen at very different ages.

Elizabeth Montagu

To be 70 years young is sometimes far more cheerful and hopeful than to be 40 years old.

Oliver Wendell Holmes Jr.

The old believe everything;
The middle-aged suspect everything;
The young know everything.

Oscar Wilde

He who laughs most, learns best.

John Cleese

Wherever there is power, there is age. Don't be deceived by dimples and curls. I tell you that babe is a thousand years old.

Ralph Waldo Emerson

Error is acceptable as long as we are young; but one must not drag it along into old age.

Johann Wolfgang von Goethe

Sagacity

Adulthood is the ever-shrinking period between childhood and old age. It is the apparent aim of modern industrial societies to reduce this period to a minimum.

Thomas Szasz

Many talents preserve their precociousness right into old age.

Karl Kraus

All the world's a stage and most of us are desperately unrehearsed.

Sean O'Casey

What do I know of man's destiny? I could tell you more about radishes.

Samuel Beckett

Few people think more than two or three times a year; I have made an international reputation for myself by thinking once or twice a week.

George Bernard Shaw

If at first you don't succeed, failure may be your style.

Quentin Crisp

Honest criticism is hard to take, particularly from a relative, a friend, an acquaintance or a stranger.

Franklin P. Jones

70 per cent of success in life is showing up.

Woody Allen

If you can't convince them, confuse them.

Harry S. Truman

A positive attitude may not solve all your problems, but it will annoy enough people to make it worth the effort.

Herm Albright

Misers aren't much fun to live with, but they do make wonderful ancestors.

Anon

Past is past and we must live the present to survive the future.

Martin Ducavne

The future is assured. It's just the past that keeps changing.

Russian joke

May the best of your past be the worst of your future.

Anon

The past is history; the future is a mystery; this moment is a gift; that is why this moment is called the present; enjoy it.

Allan Johnson

Sagacity

Know what's weird? Day by day, nothing seems to change, but pretty soon… everything's different.

Calvin, Calvin and Hobbes

Imagination was given to man to compensate him for what he isn't. A sense of humour was provided to console him for what he is.

Horace Walpole

You were born an original. Don't die a copy.

John Mason

To be able to feel the lightest touch really is a gift.

Christopher Reeve

If women ran the world we wouldn't have wars, just intense negotiations every 28 days.

Robin Williams

If you think before you speak the other guy gets his joke in first.

Jimmy Nail

For a happy and successful life you need a love of people and a love of maths.

Johnny Ball

If you obey all the rules, you miss all the fun.

Katharine Hepburn

People always call it luck when you've acted more sensibly than they have.

Anne Tyler

You don't stop laughing when you grow old; you grow old when you stop laughing.

Anon

Women on Ageing

I have to be careful to get out before I become the grotesque caricature of a hatchet-faced woman with big knockers.

Jamie Lee Curtis

I shall not grow conservative with age.

Elizabeth Cady Stanton

No one can avoid ageing, but ageing productively is something else.

Katherine Graham

A woman my age is not supposed to be attractive or sexually appealing. I just get kinda tired of that.

Kathleen Turner

Women on Ageing

At last now you can be what the old cannot recall
and the young long for in dreams, yet still include
them all.

Elizabeth Jennings

When I passed 40 I dropped pretence, 'cause men
like women who got some sense.

Maya Angelou

A woman's always younger than a man at equal
years.

Elizabeth Barrett Browning

Old age, believe me, is a good and pleasant thing. It
is true you are gently shouldered off the stage, but
then you are given such a comfortable front stall as
spectator.

Jane Harrison

You couldn't live 82 years in the world without
being disillusioned.

Rebecca West, at age 82

I do resent that when you're in the most cool,
powerful time of your life, which is your 40s,
you're put out to pasture. I think women are so
much cooler when they're older. So it's a drag that
we're not allowed to age.

Rosanna Arquette

I am really looking forward as I get older and older, to being less and less nice.

Annette Bening

When you're young, you just go right along. When you're older, you think, they've switched the rules on me.

Linda Evans

You know, when I first went into the movies Lionel Barrymore played my grandfather. Later he played my father and finally he played my husband. If he had lived I'm sure I would have played his mother. That's the way it is in Hollywood. The men get younger and the women get older.

Lillian Gish

The older I get the more of my mother I see in myself.

Nancy Friday

You take your life in your own hands, and what happens? A terrible thing: no one to blame.

Erica Jong

I spend most of my time puffing up my ego... till I'm this big ego thing... but it doesn't take much for it to be pricked, and then I'm just this deflated, shrivelled, shamed old woman with a bit of wee running down my legs.

Jenny Eclair, Grumpy Old Women

Women on Ageing

I have become more vocal in my complaining. I now say, 'This is not working for me.' This is my new sentence... It's just letting them know it's all about you, and for you, it's not working.

India Knight, Grumpy Old Women

I do write a hell of a lot of letters of complaint. I haven't really got time to do it, but I find it gets rid of some of my rage.

Sheila Hancock, Grumpy Old Women

Life is more interesting. When you're self-involved and you see yourself centre stage all the time, you're in agonies of self-consciousness, you're really concerned: how do I look? How do I sound? It's wonderful not to care about that any more.

Germaine Greer

You end up as you deserve. In old age you must put up with the face, the friends, the health, and the children you have earned.

Fay Weldon

Do not deprive me of my age. I have earned it.

May Sarton

Being 70 is not a sin.

Golda Meir

# Women on Ageing

One of the many things nobody ever tells you about middle age is that it's such a nice change from being young.

Dorothy Canfield Fisher

It is not all bad, this getting old, ripening. After the fruit has got its growth it should juice up and mellow. God forbid I should live long enough to ferment and rot and fall to the ground in a squash.

Emily Carr

As a lady of a certain age, I am willing to let the photographers and their zoom lenses stay, but only if they use their Joan Collins lens on me for close-ups.

Kay Ullrich

Every woman over 50 should stay in bed until noon.

Mamie Eisenhower

I've had to tone it down a bit. But I've still got fabulous legs and wear mini-skirts. I'll keep wearing bikinis till I'm 80... I will grow old gracefully in public – and disgracefully in private.

Jerry Hall

Men on Ageing

I don't want to be the oldest performer in captivity… I don't want to look like a little old man dancing out there.

Fred Astaire

When our memories outweigh our dreams, we have grown old.

Bill Clinton

That sign of old age, extolling the past at the expense of the present.

Sydney Smith

Men become old, but they never become good.

Oscar Wilde

As men get older, their toys get more expensive.

Marvin Davis

You get older and suddenly you don't have to go out and do all that sh★t you do when you're young and dumb. Because now you're old and dumb instead.

Johnny Depp

Old age, calm, expanded, broad with the haughty breadth of the universe, old age flowing free with the delicious near-by freedom of death.

Walt Whitman

When they came with the collection plate, they walked right past me like I was a penniless mugger.

Jimmy Savile, on attending Christmas Mass

The older we grow, the greater become the ordeals.

Johann Wolfgang von Goethe

A man over 90 is a great comfort to all his elderly neighbours: he is a picket-guard at the extreme outpost; and the young folks of 60 and 70 feel that the enemy must get by him before he can come near their camp.

Oliver Wendell Holmes

I've been grumpy since the age of 10, so it wasn't a generational shift.

I never expect anything to get better. I just am grumpy.

Sir Bob Geldof

I didn't turn into, at the age of 30, a grumpy old man, I was a grumpy teenager as well.

Rory McGrath

Every man desires to live long; but no man would be old.

Jonathan Swift

Men on Ageing

I think a lot about getting old. I don't want to be one of those 70-year-olds who still want lots of sex.

Rupert Everett

If we spent as much time feeling positive about getting older, as we do trying to stay young, how much different our lives would be.

Rob Brown

I think when the full horror of being 50 hits you; you should stay home and have a good cry.

Alan Bleasdale

Perhaps being old is having lighted rooms inside your head, and people in them, acting. People you know yet can't quite name.

Philip Larkin

I have found it to be true that the older I've become the better my life has become.

Rush Limbaugh

I think in 20 years I'll be looked at like Bob Hope. Doing those president jokes and golf sh★t. It scares me.

Eddie Murphy

At my age, I want to wake up and see sunshine pouring in through the windows every day.

John Cleese

Age is not a particularly interesting subject. Anyone can get old. All you have to do is live long enough.

Groucho Marx

Some mornings, it's just not worth chewing through the leather straps.

Emo Philips

As I get older I seem to believe less and less and yet to believe what I do believe more and more.

Gerald Brenan

You feel a little older in the morning. By noon I feel about 55.

Bob Dole

I still find each day too short for all the thoughts I want to think, all the walks I want to take, all the books I want to read, and all the friends I want to see.

John Burroughs

The more defects a man may have, the older he is, the less lovable, the more resounding his success.

Marquis de Sade

Few people know how to be old.

François de La Rochefoucauld

Men on Ageing

Most men do not mature, they simply grow taller.

Leo Rosten

I am my age. I'm not making any effort to change it.

Harrison Ford

The older I get, the more I become an apple pie, sparkling cider kind of guy.

Scott Foley

A man can be much amused when he hears himself seriously called an old man for the first time.

T. Kinnes

Age is how you feel. If you take care of yourself, you'll be able to do the same things. You may not do it as often. But you can still do it.

Barry Bonds

Nobody went out to pasture, and a lot of people are doing their best work. Bruce Springsteen, Tom Petty and Sting are at the top of their game. I mean, Tony Bennett is the coolest guy I ever met! We have to figure out how to break out of this age ghetto.

Bonnie Raitt

I know I can't cheat death, but I can cheat old age.

Darwin Deason

I like men who have a future and women who
have a past.

Oscar Wilde

As one grows older one must try not to work
oneself to death unnecessarily. At least that's how it
is with me... I can scarcely keep pace and must
watch out that the creative forces do not chase me
around the universe in a wallop.

Carl Jung

Men of my age live in a state of continual
desperation.

Trevor McDonald

Old age is an insult. It's like being smacked.

Lawrence Durrell

Old age: I fall asleep during the funerals of my
friends.

Mason Cooley

I don't think I've gotten any smarter, but your
reflexes slow down before you do something
stupid when you're older.

Kris Kristofferson

I'm only two years older than Brad Pitt, but I look
a lot older, which used to greatly frustrate me. It
doesn't any more.

George Clooney

Listen to Your Elders

They're of a certain age, these ladies. You know, past their procreational best.

> *Ian McCaskill*, discussing his admirers

Old age scares me. Almost everyone I know who is old is quite miserable, especially men.

> *Rupert Everett*

Listen to Your Elders

Look to the future, because that is where you'll spend the rest of your life.

> *George Burns*

Don't take life too seriously; you'll never get out of it alive.

> *Elbert Hubbard*

You can add years to your life by wearing your pants backwards.

> *Johnny Carson*

Don't smoke too much, drink too much, eat too much or work too much. We're all on the road to the grave – but there's no need to be in the passing lane.

> *Robert Orben*

Stay humble. Always answer your phone – no matter who else is in the car.

Jack Lemmon

My mum died about three years ago at the age of 101, and just towards the end, as she began to run out of energy, she did actually stop trying to tell me what to do most of the time.

John Cleese

Forget past mistakes. Forget failures. Forget everything except what you are going to do now and do it.

William Durant

Do not do unto others as you expect they should do unto you; their tastes may not be the same.

George Bernard Shaw

First law on holes – when you're in one, stop digging.

Denis Healey

If at first you don't succeed, try, try again. Then quit. No use being a damn fool about it.

W.C. Fields

How people keep correcting us when we are young! There is always some bad habit or other they tell us we ought to get over. Yet most bad habits are tools to help us through life.

Jack Nicklaus

Listen to Your Elders

It is better to die on your feet than to live on your knees.

Dolores Ibarruri

The time to begin most things is 10 years ago.

Mignon McLaughlin

Never think you've seen the last of anything.

Eudora Welty

There are times not to flirt. When you're sick. When you're with children. When you're on the witness stand.

Joyce Jillson

Be bold. If you're going to make an error, make a doozey, and don't be afraid to hit the ball.

Billie Jean King

Find an aim in life before you run out of ammunition.

Arnold Glasow

I don't know the key to success, but the key to failure is trying to please everybody.

Bill Cosby

Always read stuff that will make you look good if you die in the middle of it.

P.J. O'Rourke

Never kick a fresh turd on a hot day.

Harry S. Truman

Be careful about reading health books. You might die of a misprint.

Mark Twain

Take the goods the gods provide, and don't stand and sulk when they are snatched away.

Mary McMullen

Go through your phone book, call people and ask them to drive you to the airport. The ones who will drive you are your true friends. The rest aren't bad people; they're just acquaintances.

Jay Leno

Be equal to your talent, not your age. At times let the gap between them be embarrassing.

Yevgeny Yevtushenko

At 46 one must be a miser; only have time for essentials.

Virginia Woolf

You can't have everything. Where would you put it?

Steven Wright

In real life, I assure you, there is no such thing as algebra.

Fran Lebowitz

Listen to Your Elders

Sometimes the road less travelled is less travelled for a reason.

Jerry Seinfeld

Never pick a fight with an ugly person, they've got nothing to lose.

Robin Williams

You can observe a lot just by watching.

Yogi Berra

There are only two ways of telling the complete truth – anonymously and posthumously.

Thomas Sowell

When you get to the end of your rope, tie a knot and hang on.

Franklin D. Roosevelt

Don't worry about the world coming to an end today. It's already tomorrow in Australia.

Charles M. Schulz

Be who you are and say what you feel, because those who mind don't matter and those who matter don't mind.

Dr. Seuss

You're only given a little spark of madness. You mustn't lose it.

Robin Williams

Son, always tell the truth. Then you'll never have to remember what you said the last time.

Sam Rayburn

Whatever you want to do, do it now. There are only so many tomorrows.

Michael Landon

Golden Oldies

FAMOUS OLDIES

I have enjoyed greatly the second blooming that comes when you finish the life of the emotions and of personal relations; and suddenly find – at the age of 50, say – that a whole new life has opened before you, filled with things you can think about, study, or read about… It is as if a fresh sap of ideas and thoughts was rising in you.

Agatha Christie

When you're a young man, Macbeth is a character part. When you're older, it's a straight part.

Laurence Olivier

Golden Oldies

Old age is like everything else. To make a success of it, you've got to start young.

Fred Astaire

I have the body of an 18-year-old. I keep it in the fridge.

Spike Milligan

One of the advantages of ageing is losing obsession about work and being able to spend some more time with your family.

Clint Eastwood

In his later years Pablo Picasso was not allowed to roam an art gallery unattended, for he had previously been discovered in the act of trying to improve on one of his old masterpieces.

Anon

You can't be as old as I am without waking up with a surprised look on your face every morning: 'Holy Christ, what da ya know – I'm still around!' It's absolutely amazing that I survived all the booze and smoking and the cars and the career.

Paul Newman

I used to desire many, many things, but now I have just one desire, and that's to get rid of all my other desires.

John Cleese

I shall not waste my days in trying to prolong them.

Ian L. Fleming

These days I am a teetotal, mean-spirited, right-wing, narrow-minded, conservative Christian bigot, but not a racist.

Jane Russell, speaking in 2003

I look forward to being older, when what you look like becomes less and less an issue and what you are is the point.

Susan Sarandon

Hollywood will accept actresses playing 10 years older, but actors can play 10 years younger.

Greta Scacchi

I have no regrets. I wouldn't have lived my life the way I did if I was going to worry about what people were going to say.

Ingrid Bergman

At my age I do what Mark Twain did. I get my daily paper, look at the obituaries page and if I'm not there I carry on as usual.

Patrick Moore

I feel like an old geezer!... Well, I am an old geezer.

Terry Wogan

Golden Oldies

I am affectionately known by Elton John as either Sylvia Disc or the Bionic Christian.

Sir Cliff Richard

In two years time I will be 50. But age doesn't hold any terrors for me because I feel stronger than ever.

Pierce Brosnan

I am not young enough to know everything.

Oscar Wilde

I will never give in to old age until I become old. And I'm not old yet!

Tina Turner

Getting old is a fascination thing. The older you get, the older you want to get.

Keith Richards

With 60 staring me in the face, I have developed inflammation of the sentence structure and a definite hardening of the paragraphs.

James Thurber

I love life because what more is there.

Anthony Hopkins

I am not the first man who wanted to make changes in his life at 60 and I won't be the last. It is just that others can do it with anonymity.

Harrison Ford

Everyone says I'm terrified of getting old but the truth is that in my job becoming old and extinct are one and the same thing.

Cher

My mother, God rest her soul, as soon as you gave her something, she would be eyeing it up to see who she could give it to when they turned up and she didn't have a present for them. You could see the virtual wrapping paper going around the thing you bought… you could see it was on its way to Doris next door.

Maureen Lipman, Grumpy Old Women

No sophisticated time schedule any more, that is something marvellous. Just cooking noodles, cultivating tomatoes, playing golf, lying in bed, eating chips with ketchup and spooning up peanut butter directly from the glass.

Celine Dion

I will actually say, 'Look, I'm very old and I'm very bored with you all, and I'm leaving.' It's one of the advantages of ageing – you can be eccentric and rude.

Sheila Hancock, Grumpy Old Women

Golden Oldies

Wouldn't it be great if people could get to live suddenly as often as they die suddenly?

Katharine Hepburn

Professionally, I have no age.

Kathleen Turner

I think I'm finally growing up – and about time.

Elizabeth Taylor

It is far better to be out with beautiful girls than be an old fart in the pub talking about what you were like in the 60s.

Mick Jagger

There are very little things in this life I cannot afford and patience is one of them.

Larry Hagman

Because young men are so goddamn disappointing!

Harrison Ford, explaining why women like older leading men

Things hurt me now. My knees hurt, my back hurts. But your head still thinks it's 23.

George Clooney

Harrison Ford may be getting old, but he can fight like a 28-year-old man.

Harrison Ford

Golfing Grandpas

If you watch a game, it's fun. If you play it, it's recreation. If you work at it, it's golf.

Bob Hope

Golf is a good walk spoiled.

Mark Twain

Golf is more fun than walking naked in a strange place, but not much.

Buddy Hackett

Playing golf is like going to a strip joint. After 18 holes you're tired and most of your balls are missing.

Tim Allen

The uglier a man's legs are, the better he plays golf – it's almost a law.

H. G. Wells

Golf is a fascinating game. It has taken me nearly 40 years to discover that I can't play it.

Ted Ray

When I die, bury me on the golf course so my husband will visit.

Anon

I would like to deny all allegations by Bob Hope that during my last game of golf, I hit an eagle, a birdie, an elk and a moose.

Gerald Ford

I'll shoot my age if I have to live to be 105.

Bob Hope

The only time my prayers are never answered is on the golf course.

Billy Graham

Sex and golf are the two things you can enjoy even if you're not good at them.

Kevin Costner

I know I'm getting better at golf because I'm hitting fewer spectators.

Gerald Ford

Eric: My wife says if I don't give up golf, she'll leave me.
Ernie: That's terrible.
Eric: I know – I'm really going to miss her.

Eric Morecombe and Ernie Wise

It was cool for a couple of weeks, but how much bad golf can you play?

John Goodman

It took me 17 years to get 3,000 hits in baseball. I did it in one afternoon on the golf course.

Hank Aaron

I had a wonderful experience on the golf course today. I had a hole in nothing. Missed the ball and sank the divot.

Don Adams

In the Bob Hope Golf Classic, the participation of President Gerald Ford was more than enough to remind you that the nuclear button was at one stage at the disposal of a man who might have either pressed it by mistake or else pressed it deliberately in order to obtain room service.

Clive James

The only way to enjoy golf is to be a masochist. Go out and beat yourself to death.

Howard Keel

If you think it's hard to meet new people, try picking up the wrong golf ball.

Jack Lemmon

If I wasn't an actor I'd be unemployable, or at best the secretary to a golf club somewhere. Nine holes at that, and blue in the face with port.

David Niven

Golfing Grandpas

I can't hit a ball more than 200 yards. I have no butt. You need a butt if you're going to hit a golf ball.

Dennis Quaid

I'm patient with crossword puzzles and the most impatient golfer.

Brett Hull

Golf is a day spent in a round of strenuous idleness.

William Wordsworth

I would rather play *Hamlet* with no rehearsal than TV golf.

Jack Lemmon

If you are caught on a golf course during a storm and are afraid of lightning, hold up a 1-iron. Not even God can hit a 1-iron.

Lee Trevino

Sport is a wonderful metaphor for life. Of all the sports that I played – skiing, baseball, fishing – there is no greater example than golf, because you're playing against yourself and nature.

Robert Redford

I don't have a life, I really don't. I'm as close to a nun as you can be without the little hat. I'm a golf nun.

Gabrielle Reece

In my retirement I go for a short swim at least once or twice every day. It's either that or buy a new golf ball.

Gene Perret

The reason the pro tells you to keep your head down is so you can't see him laughing.

Phyllis Diller

If you drink, don't drive. Don't even putt.

Dean Martin

If you are going to throw a club, it is important to throw it ahead of you, down the fairway, so you don't have to waste energy going back to pick it up.

Tommy Bolt

Acting has been good to me. It's taken me to play golf all over the world.

Christopher Lee

It is almost impossible to remember how tragic a place the world is when one is playing golf.

Robert Lynd

Geriatric Gardening

Long ago, when men cursed and beat the ground with sticks, it was called witchcraft. Today, it's called golf.

Anon

Golf: a game where white men can dress up as black pimps and get away with it.

Robin Williams

The golf course is the only place I can go dressed like a pimp and fit in perfectly. Anywhere else, lime-green pants and alligator shoes, I got a cop on my ass.

Samuel L. Jackson

I'm a coloured, one-eyed Jew… do I need anything else?

Sammy Davis Jr., in answer to a question: What's your golf handicap?

The place of the father in the modern suburban family is a very small one, particularly if he plays golf.

Bertrand Russell

Geriatric Gardening

To get the best results you must talk to your vegetables.

Prince Charles

Geriatric Gardening

Though an old man, I am but a young gardener.

Thomas Jefferson

I want Death to find me planting my cabbages.

Michel De Montaigne

Planting is one of my great amusements, and even of those things which can only be for posterity, for a Septuagenary has no right to count on any thing but annuals.

Thomas Jefferson

If you want to be happy for a short time, get drunk; happy for a long time, fall in love; happy forever, take up gardening.

Arthur Smith

Live each day as if it were your last, and garden as though you will live forever.

Anon

What a man needs in gardening is a cast-iron back, with a hinge in it.

Charles Dudley Warner

In gardens, beauty is a by-product. The main business is sex and death.

Sam Llewellyn

Geriatric Gardening

Then again, if the plant is slow growing, and you are getting older, you may want to start with a larger plant. I find myself buying larger plants each year.

Bill Cannon

Cherry trees will blossom every year; but I'll disappear for good, one of these days.

Philip Whalen

We come from the earth, we return to the earth, and in between we garden.

Anon

Everything ends with flowers.

Hélène Cixous

If you are not killing plants, you are not really stretching yourself as a gardener.

J. C. Raulston

When gardening, I have one gift you won't find in any manuals. I know it's strange, but I can change perennials to annuals.

Dick Emmons

Old gardeners never die. They just spade away and then throw in the trowel.

Herbert V. Prochnow

I'm not ageing, I just need re-potting.

Anon

Now the gardener is the one who has seen everything ruined so many times that (even as his pain increases with each loss) he comprehends – truly knows – that where there was a garden once, it can be again, or where there never was, there yet can be a garden.

Henry Mitchell

40 is about the age for unexpected developments: extroverts turn introspective, introverts become sociable, and everyone, without regard to type, acquires grey hairs and philosophies of life. Many also acquire gardens.

Janice Emily Bowens

Spicing up the Twilight Years

Once the travel bug bites there is no known antidote, and I know that I shall be happily infected until the end of my life.

Michael Palin

Football and cookery are the two most important subjects in this country.

Delia Smith

Spicing up the Twilight Years

Life may not be the party we hoped for, but while we are here we might as well dance.

J.Williams

Give a man a fish and he has food for a day. Teach him how to fish and you can get rid of him for the entire weekend.

Zenna Schaffer

One of the worst things that can happen in life is to win a bet on a horse at an early age.

Danny McGoorty, Irish pool player

If people concentrated on the really important things in life, there'd be a shortage of fishing poles.

Doug Larson

There is a very fine line between 'hobby' and 'mental illness'.

Dave Barry

Hell, if I'd jumped on all the dames I'm supposed to have jumped on, I'd have had no time to go fishing.

Clark Gable

I go to Alaska and fish salmon. I do some halibut fishing, lake fishing, trout fishing, fly fishing. I look quite good in waders. I love my waders. I don't think there is anything sexier than just standing in waders with a fly rod. I just love it.

Linda Hamilton

I only make movies to finance my fishing.

Lee Marvin

Fishing is boring, unless you catch an actual fish, and then it is disgusting.

Dave Barry

I'm always suspicious of games where you're the only ones that play it.

Jack Charlton, on hurling

Skiing consists of wearing $3,000 worth of clothes and equipment and driving 200 miles in the snow in order to stand around at a bar and drink.

P. J. O'Rourke

There's a fine line between fishing and just standing on the shore like an idiot.

Steven Wright

Skiing combines outdoor fun with knocking down trees with your face.

Dave Barry

I'm Gonna Live Forever

The secret of longevity is to keep breathing.

Sophie Tucker

If man were immortal, do you realise what his meat bills would be?

Woody Allen

To lengthen thy life, lessen thy meals.

Benjamin Franklin

The secret to a long life is to stay busy, get plenty of exercise, and don't drink too much. Then again, don't drink too little.

Hermann Smith-Johansson, at age 103

Pretend to be dumb, that's the only way to reach old age.

Friedrich Dürrenmatt

A man 90 years old was asked to what he attributed his longevity.

'I reckon', he said, with a twinkle in his eye, 'it's because most nights I went to bed and slept when I should have sat up and worried.'

Dorothea Kent

If you live to the age of a hundred you've made it because very few people die past the age of a hundred.

George Burns

My formula for living is quite simple. I get up in the morning and I go to bed at night. In between, I occupy myself as best I can.

Cary Grant

The only real way to look younger is not to be born so soon.

Charles M. Schulz

I've already lived about 20 years longer than my life expectancy at the time I was born. That's a source of annoyance to a great many people.

Ronald Reagan

I wanna live 'til I die, no more, no less.

Eddie Izzard

He had decided to live forever or die in the attempt.

Joseph Heller

Ageing seems to be the only available way to live a long life.

Daniel Auber

I'm Gonna Live Forever

Roz: Physical contact extends our lives.
Frasier: Well then, you'll outlive Styrofoam.

Frasier

There is a fountain of youth: it is your mind, your talents, the creativity you bring to your life and the lives of the people you love. When you learn to tap this source, you will truly have defeated age.

Sophia Loren

I postpone death by living, by suffering, by error, by risking, by giving, by losing.

Anais Nin

I am long on ideas, but short on time. I expect to live to be only about a hundred.

Thomas Alva Edison

We could certainly slow the ageing process down if it had to work its way through Congress.

Anon

My secret for staying young is good food, plenty of rest, and a make-up man with a spray gun.

Bob Hope

I'd like to grow very old as slowly as possible.

Irene Mayer Selznick

My only fear is that I may live too long. This would be a subject of dread to me.

Thomas Jefferson

I would not live forever, because we should not live forever, because if we were supposed to live forever, then we would live forever, but we cannot live forever, which is why I would not live forever.

Miss Alabama, 1994 Miss USA contest

Porridge is also the secret to a long life. I have it in the morning and it's the best start to the day.

Anon

Many Happy Returns

Most of us can remember a time when a birthday, especially if it was one's own, brightened the world as if a second sun had risen.

Robert Lynd

It is lovely, when I forget all birthdays, including my own, to find that somebody remembers me.

Ellen Glasgow

The formula for youth: Keep your enthusiasm and forget your birthdays.

Anon

Don't send funny greeting cards on birthdays or at Christmas. Save them for funerals when their cheery effect is needed.

P.J. O'Rourke

What ought to be done to the man who invented the celebrating of anniversaries? Mere killing would be too light.

Mark Twain

I always add a year to myself, so I'm prepared for my next birthday. So when I was 39, I was already 40.

Nicolas Cage

When I was a kid I could toast marshmallows over my birthday candles. Now I could roast a turkey!

Anon

There comes a time when you should stop expecting other people to make a big deal about your birthday. That time is age 11.

Dave Barry

Is that a birthday? 'Tis, alas! too clear; 'tis but the funeral of the former year.

Alexander Pope

You Can Teach an Old Dog New Tricks

When a man has a birthday, he takes a day off.
When a woman has a birthday, she takes at least
three years off.

Joan Rivers

The best birthdays of all are those that haven't
arrived yet.

Robert Orben

From our birthday, until we die, is but the winking
of an eye.

William Butler Yeats

Last year my birthday cake looked like a prairie fire.

Rodney Dangerfield

You Can Teach an Old Dog New Tricks

When I was young I was amazed at Plutarch's
statement that the elder Cato began at the age of
80 to learn Greek. I am amazed no longer. Old age
is ready to undertake tasks that youth shirked
because they would take too long.

W. Somerset Maugham

I enjoy going to the centre because I always get a
lovely smile from the ladies there and I can impress
them with new computer tips.

Lady, 100, attending computer classes

You are never too old. One of many examples,
Grandma Moses (1860–1961), she started
painting in her late 70s. She is best known for
her documentary paintings of rural life. If you
ever think you are too old, think of Grandma
Moses!

Catherine Pulsifer

You are never too old to set another goal or to
dream a new dream.

Les Brown

I'm having difficulty getting the doctors around
here to sign the appropriate form.

Spike Milligan, on seeking permission to celebrate his
eightieth birthday with a 12,000 foot skydive.

Retirement is a Dirty Word

Retirement at 65 is ridiculous. When I was 65 I
still had pimples.

George Burns

Retirement is a Dirty Word

Never retire. Michelangelo was carving the *Rondanini* just before he died at 89. Verdi finished his opera *Falstaff* at 80. And the 80-year-old artist Goya scrawled on a drawing, 'I am still learning'.

Dr. W. Gifford-Jones

On announcing his retirement: You can only milk a cow for so long, then you're left holding the pail.

Hank Aaron

I'm mad, you know? I don't think of retiring at all.

Paul McCartney

People are always asking me when I'm going to retire. Why should I? I'm still making movies, and I'm a senior citizen, so I can see myself at half price.

George Burns

This is my final word. It is time for me to become an apprentice once more. I have not settled in which direction. But somewhere, sometime, soon.

Lord Beaverbrook, taken from his last public statement

Retirement is a Dirty Word

I don't want to retire. I'm not that good at crossword puzzles.

Norman Mailer

When old, retire from work, but not from life.

M.K. Soni

If youth is wasted on the young, then retirement is wasted on the old.

Anon

Retire? I'm going to stay in show business until I'm the only one left.

George Burns, age 90

At 85 you can only think ahead for the next 50 years or so.

Chuck Jones, on signing a long-term contract with Warner Brothers

Don't retire, retread!

Robert Otterbourg

Retirement is the period when you exchange the bills in your wallet for snapshots of your grandchildren.

Anon

Retirement is a Dirty Word

It's been different. I started driving again. I started cooking again. My driving's better than my cooking. George has discovered Sam's Club.

Barbara Bush

When a man retires and time is no longer a matter of urgent importance, his colleagues generally present him with a watch.

R. C. Sherriff

Retirement: That's when you return from work one day and say, 'Hi, honey, I'm home – forever.'

Gene Perret

You're 65 today – and it's the first day of the rest of your life savings.

Anon

Retirement? You're talking about death, right?

Robert Altman

Retirement kills more people than hard work ever did.

Malcolm Forbes

The trouble with retirement is that you never get a day off.

Abe Lemons

Retirement is a Dirty Word

I'm retired – goodbye tension, hello pension!

Anon

When a man retires, his wife gets twice the
husband but only half the income.

Chi Chi Rodriguez

Retired is being twice tired, I've thought. First
tired of working, then tired of not.

Richard Armour

Retirement: It's nice to get out of the rat race, but
you have to learn to get along with less cheese.

Gene Perret

I love working. It's what I do best, and if I didn't
work and tried to slow down, I'd just become a
boring old fart.

Rik Mayall

Middle age is when work is a lot less fun and fun is
a lot more work.

Anon

O, blest retirement! friend to life's decline –
How blest is he who crowns, in shades like these,
A youth of labour with an age of ease!

Oliver Goldsmith

Retirement is a Dirty Word

Retirement is wonderful. It's doing nothing without worrying about getting caught at it.

Gene Perret

There are some who start their retirement long before they stop working.

Robert Half

The question isn't at what age I want to retire, it's at what income.

George Foreman

The challenge of retirement is how to spend time without spending money.

Anon

Once it was impossible to find any Bond villains older than myself, I retired.

Roger Moore

Retirement means no pressure, no stress, no heartache... unless you play golf.

Gene Perret

Retirement must be wonderful. I mean, you can suck in your stomach for only so long.

Burt Reynolds

When you retire, think and act as if you were still working; when you're still working, think and act a bit as if you were already retired.

Anon

I've been trying for some time to develop a lifestyle that doesn't require my presence.

Gary Trudeau

Retirement – now life begins.

Catherine Pulsifer

Crowning Glory

By common consent, grey hairs are a crown of glory: the only object of respect that can never excite envy.

George Bancroft

There is only one cure for grey hair. It was invented by a Frenchman. It is called the guillotine.

P.G. Wodehouse

It is not by the grey of the hair that one knows the age of the heart.

Edward Bulwer-Lytton

It seems no more than right that men should seize time by the forelock, for the rude old fellow, sooner or later, pulls all their hair out.

George Dennison Prentice

There is more felicity on the far side of baldness than young men can possibly imagine.

Logan Pearsall Smith

Inflation is when you pay $15 for the $10 haircut you used to get for five dollars when you had hair.

Sam Ewing

Grey hair is God's graffiti.

Bill Cosby

I'm entering the 'metallic years'; silver in my hair, gold in my teeth and lead in my bottom!

Anon

André Gide was very bald with the general look of an elderly fallen angel travelling incognito.

Peter Quennell

On the bright side of life you will probably save a lot on shampoo when getting old and bald, and no longer have to suffer from thwarted and long gone ambitions.

T. Kinnes

Crowning Glory

After watching Cary Grant on a television broadcast, his mother, then in her 90s, reprimanded him for letting his hair get so grey. 'It doesn't bother me,' the actor replied carelessly. 'Maybe not,' said his mother, 'but it bothers *me*. It makes me seem so old.'

Anon

The best thing about being bald is when her folks come home; all you have to do is straighten your tie.

Milton Berle

He wore his baldness like an expensive hat.

Gloria Swanson

My husband was bending over to tie my three-year-old's shoes. That's when I noticed my son Ben staring at my husband's head. He gently touched the slightly thinning spot of hair and said in a concerned voice, 'Daddy, you have a hole in your head. Does it hurt?' After a pause, I heard my husband's murmured reply, 'Not physically.'

Reader's Digest

Women love a self-confident bald man.

Larry David

Crowning Glory

I'm not really bald. I just have a very wide parting.

Anon

The tenderest spot in a man's make-up is sometimes the bald spot on top of his head.

Helen Rowland

Violet will be a good colour for hair at just about the same time that brunette becomes a good colour for flowers.

Fran Lebowitz

The simple truth is that balding African-American men look cool when they shave their heads, whereas balding white men look like giant thumbs.

Dave Barry

Grey hairs are signs of wisdom if you hold your tongue. Speak and they are but hairs, as in the young.

Anon

We're all born bald, baby.

Telly Savalas

I feel old when I see mousse in my opponent's hair.

Andre Agassi

Crowning Glory

I'm not bald... I'm just taller than my hair.

Clive Anderson

I know body hair bothers some women, but a lot of men like a fluffy partner.

Dame Edna Everage

You can always tell where Diana Ross has been by the hair that's left behind!

Diana Ross

The secret of my success is my hairspray.

Richard Gere

A man is usually bald four or five years before he knows it.

Ed Howe

The worst thing a man can do is go bald. Never let yourself go bald.

Donald Trump

He's the kind of guy that when he dies, he's going up to heaven and give God a bad time for making him bald.

Marlon Brando, on Frank Sinatra

It's a question that I find like asking somebody, 'Did you have a breast implant?' or 'When did you get your lobotomy?

William Shatner, when asked if he wore a hairpiece

My hairdresser actually spends more time digging hair out of my ears than off the top or back of my head.

Des Lynam, Grumpy Old Men

When others kid me about being bald, I simply tell them that the way I figure it, the good Lord only gave men so many hormones, and if others want to waste theirs on growing hair, that's up to them.

John Glenn

A hair in the head is worth two in the brush.

Don Herold

Teething Troubles

I had very good dentures once. Some magnificent gold work. It's the only form of jewellery a man can wear that women fully appreciate.

Graham Greene

Dentures: Two rows of artificial ivories that may be removed periodically to frighten one's grandchildren or provide accompaniment to Spanish music.

Anon

It is after you have lost your teeth that you can afford to buy steaks.

Pierre Auguste Renoir

Teething Troubles

We idolised the Beatles, except for those of us who idolised the Rolling Stones, who in those days still had many of their original teeth.

Dave Barry

I've gotten to the age where I need my false teeth and hearing aid before I can ask where I left my glasses.

Anon

I don't have false teeth. Do you think I'd buy teeth like these?

Carol Burnett

Every tooth in a man's head is more valuable than a diamond.

Miguel de Cervantes

I like my bifocals,
my dentures fit me fine,
my hearing aid is perfect,
but Lord I miss my mind!

Anon

She had so many gold teeth... she used to have to sleep with her head in a safe.

W.C. Fields

Now Bart, since you broke Grandpa's teeth, he gets to break yours.

Homer Simpson, The Simpsons

The good news about mid-life is that the glass is still half-full. Of course, the bad news is that it won't be long before your teeth are floating in it.

Anon

Ribs, great... why don't you just kick the dentures out of my mouth?

Sophia Petrillo, The Golden Girls

I swear if Colgate comes out with one more type of toothpaste. I just want clean teeth; that's all I want. I don't want the tartar and I don't want the cavities. And I want white teeth. How come I have to choose? And then they have the 'Colgate Total' that supposedly has everything in there. I don't believe that for one second. If it's all in the one, how come they make all the others? Who's going: 'I don't mind the tartar so much'?

Ellen DeGeneres

God gives nuts to those with no teeth.

Anon

I Shall Wear Purple

After 50 a man discovers he does not need more than one suit.

Clifton Fadiman

Being home on a Friday night with the old man, an Indian take-away and a nice bottle of wine, and there's something on the telly, oh, I like that. I'm in my dressing gown, I mean it's not a weird dressing gown, it's not one of those quilted old lady ones. It's Cath Kidston. It's quite a funky dressing gown... don't get me wrong. I'm not that old.

Jenny Eclair, Grumpy Old Women

If women dressed for men, the stores wouldn't sell much – just an occasional sun visor.

Groucho Marx

Underwear makes me uncomfortable and besides my parts have to breathe.

Jean Harlow

Trying on pants is one of the most humiliating things a man can suffer that doesn't involve a woman.

Larry David

You'd be surprised how much it costs to look this cheap.

Dolly Parton

I Shall Wear Purple

I am 56 years old, an age when many women tend not to be noticed as we plod about in our extra wide, midi-heeled sensible shoes.

Sue Townsend

You can say what you like about long dresses, but they cover a multitude of shins.

Mae West

She looked as if she had been poured into her clothes and had forgotten to say 'when'.

P.G. Wodehouse

Brevity is the soul of lingerie.

Dorothy Parker

Dress simply. If you wear a dinner jacket, don't wear anything else on it… like lunch or dinner.

George Burns

Nothing goes out of fashion sooner than a long dress with a very low neck.

Coco Chanel

Fashion is what you adopt when you don't know who you are.

Quentin Crisp

I Shall Wear Purple

The only man I know who behaves sensibly is my tailor; he takes my measurements anew each time he sees me. The rest go on with their old measurements and expect me to fit them.

George Bernard Shaw

If God had meant us to walk around naked, he would never have invented the wicker chair.

Erma Bombeck

Gloves complete a look. That's my belief. Who cares if I'm right or wrong? I had a mother who encouraged me to go with impulses. And I have, and it's led to some insanely ridiculous outfits, but I like it that way.

Diane Keaton

I wouldn't say I invented tacky, but I definitely brought it to its present high popularity.

Bette Midler

How on earth did Gandhi manage to walk so far in flip-flops? I can't last 10 minutes in mine.

Mrs. Merton

I don't think I would've worn thongs even when I was young and trying very hard. No, that's ridiculous. You might as well go without knickers at all.

Annette Crosbie, Grumpy Old Women

And you know, the baby boomers are getting older, and those off the rack clothes are just not fitting right any longer, and so, tailor-made suits are coming back into fashion.

Amy Irving

I base my fashion taste on what doesn't itch.

Gilda Radner

Now that I'm old [clothes shopping] has become entirely frustrating because there is nothing for me to wear in the shops. Nothing. I mean, I'm not going to wear hipster pants, am I? If I wear hipster pants and I sit down, I'll shoot out the back of them. It's not on.

Germaine Greer, Grumpy Old Women

Show me a man with both feet on the ground and I'll show you a man who can't get his pants on.

Joe E. Lewis

Tell me the history of that frock, Janet. It's obviously an old favourite. You were wise to remove the curtain rings. I love that fabric. You were lucky to find so much of it.

Dame Edna Everage

I Shall Wear Purple

Once you can accept the universe as matter expanding into nothing that is something, wearing stripes with plaid comes easy.

Albert Einstein

Women's clothes: never wear anything that panics the cat.

P.J. O'Rourke

Some women hold up dresses that are so ugly and they always say the same thing: 'This looks much better on.' On what? On fire?

Marsha Warfield

Hilary: One of the few lessons I have learned in life is that there is invariably something odd about women who wear ankle socks.

Alan Bennett, The Old Country

Fashion is a form of ugliness so intolerable that we have to alter it every six months.

Oscar Wilde

I grow old... I grow old... I shall wear the bottoms of my trousers rolled.

T.S. Eliot

I wouldn't say her bathing suit was skimpy, but I've seen more cotton in the top of an aspirin bottle.

Henny Youngman

Denise: Dad, stop fiddling with yerself.
Jim: I'm not fiddling with meself. I paid a quid for these underpants and I've got 50 pence stuck up me arse.

Denise and Jim Royle, The Royle Family

I know what Victoria's Secret is. The secret is that nobody older than 30 can fit into their stuff.

Sima Jacobson

A hat should be taken off when you greet a lady and left off for the rest of your life. Nothing looks more stupid than a hat.

P.J. O'Rourke

Though I am grateful for the blessings of wealth, it hasn't changed who I am. My feet are still on the ground. I'm just wearing better shoes.

Oprah Winfrey

I never cared for fashion much, amusing little seams and witty little pleats: it was the girls I liked.

David Bailey

Young at Heart

He says he feels young at heart but slightly older in other places.

Anon

Young at Heart

Another belief of mine: that everyone else my age is an adult, whereas I am merely in disguise.

Margaret Atwood

You can't help getting older, but you don't have to get old.

George Burns

You're only young once, but you can be immature forever.

John Greier

One starts to get young at the age of 60 and then it is too late.

Pablo Picasso

When I was 10, I read fairy tales in secret and would have been ashamed if I had been found doing so. Now that I am 50, I read them openly. When I became a man, I put away childish things – including the fear of childishness and the desire to be grown-up.

C.S. Lewis

Setting a good example for your children takes all the fun out of middle age.

William Feather

I have spent my whole life – up to a minute ago – being younger than I am now.

John Ciardi

Except for an occasional heart attack I feel as young as I ever did.

Robert Benchley

Try to keep your soul young and quivering right up to old age.

George Sand

Life would be infinitely happier if we could only be born at the age of 80 and gradually approach 18.

Mark Twain

Over the Hill

I'm so old they've cancelled my blood type.

Bob Hope

I'd rather be over the hill than under it.

Anon

To live beyond 80 is an exaggeration, almost an excess.

Antonio Callado

Over the Hill

Wrecked on the lee shore of age.

Sarah Orne Jewett

Just remember, once you're over the hill you begin to pick up speed.

Charles M. Schulz

You know you're over the hill when the only whistles you get are from the tea kettle.

Anon

The follies which a man regrets most in his life are those which he didn't commit when he had the opportunity.

Helen Rowland

I didn't get old on purpose, it just happened. If you're lucky it could happen to you.

Andy Rooney

A lot of people start to fall to bits at 30… quite honestly once you are able to reproduce you're over the hill. You start to go downhill at 18 physically.

Mick Jagger

Over the hill? I don't remember any hill?!

Anon

I'd Rather Have a Cup of Tea

I'm too beat-up and old now to be a sex symbol.

Mel Gibson

I've been around so long I can remember Doris Day before she was a virgin.

Groucho Marx

I'm too old for this sh★t!

Danny Glover, as Roger Murtaugh, Lethal Weapon

You're not over the hill until you hear your favourite songs in an elevator!

Anon

My veins are filled once a week with a Neapolitan carpet cleaner distilled from the Adriatic and I am as bald as an egg. However, I still get around and am mean to cats.

John Cheever

I'd Rather Have a Cup of Tea

Growing old is when you resent the swimsuit issue of *Sports Illustrated* because there are fewer articles to read.

George Burns

I'd Rather Have a Cup of Tea

Everyone probably thinks that I'm a raving nymphomaniac, that I have an insatiable sexual appetite, when the truth is I'd rather read a book.

Madonna

Middle age is having a choice of two temptations and choosing the one that will get you home earlier.

Dan Bennett

Now that I think of it, I wish I had been a hell-raiser when I was 30 years old. I tried it when I was 50 but I always got sleepy.

Groucho Marx

My wife is a sex object. Every time I ask for sex, she objects.

Les Dawson

I only watch *Baywatch* for the articles.

Chief Dan

They say marriages are made in Heaven. But so is thunder and lightning.

Clint Eastwood

I don't want to snog old men, with their yellow horrible teeth, old crinkly skin and hairy moles.

Cilla Black

Thank God! Now I realise I've been chained to an idiot for the last 60 years of my life!

Kingsley Amis at 70, on his lost libido

The important thing in acting is to be able to laugh and cry. If I have to cry, I think of my sex life. If I have to laugh, I think of my sex life.

Glenda Jackson

I haven't had sex in eight months. To be honest, I now prefer to go bowling.

Anon

As I get older, I just prefer to knit.

Tracey Ullman

I'm at the age where I want two girls. In case I fall asleep they will have someone to talk to.

Rodney Dangerfield

Sex is a bad thing because it rumples the clothes.

Jackie Onassis

I am happy now that Charles calls on my bedchamber less frequently than of old. As it is, I now endure but two calls a week and when I hear his steps outside my door I lie down on my bed, close my eyes, open my legs and think of England.

Lady Alice Hillingdon

All this fuss about sleeping together. For physical pleasure I'd sooner go to my dentist any day.

Evelyn Waugh

My wife only has sex with me for a purpose. Last night it was to time an egg.

Rodney Dangerfield

Forever Young

I believe in loyalty. When a woman reaches a certain age she likes, she should stick with it.

Eva Gabor

The trick is growing up without growing old.

Casey Stengel

I was wise enough to never grow up while fooling most people into believing I had.

Margaret Mead

The best thing about growing older is that it takes such a long time.

Anon

She was a handsome woman of 45 and would remain so for many years.

Anita Brookner

To win back my youth... there is nothing I wouldn't do – except take exercise, get up early, or be a useful member of the community.

Oscar Wilde

By the time I'd grown up, I naturally supposed that I'd grown up.

Eve Babitz

Being loved keeps you young.

Madonna

I'm saving that rocker for the day when I feel as old as I really am.

Dwight D. Eisenhower

I'm not denying my age, I'm embellishing my youth.

Tamara Reynolds

In an ideal world I would like to be alive until I am dead.

Sir John Harvey-Jones

Cheerfulness and contentment are great beautifiers, and are famous preservers of youthful looks.

Charles Dickens

Pushing 40? She's hanging on for dear life.

Ivy Compton-Burnett

She has discovered the secret of perpetual middle age.

Oscar Levant

The Pipe and Slipper Brigade

SMOKING

But when I don't smoke I scarcely feel as if I'm living. I don't feel as if I'm living unless I'm killing myself.

Russell Hoban

I have every sympathy with the American who was so horrified by what he had read of the effects of smoking that he gave up reading.

Henry G. Strauss

I would reintroduce smoking everywhere.

Martin Burton, head of Zippo's Circus, tells *Time Out* magazine how he would tackle being Mayor of London

I don't smoke, but I'd rather be with my pals who do than sitting alone in a pub with no people and no atmosphere.

Brian Monteith, Conservative MSP for Mid-Scotland and Fife

At least by going to the jungle I won't have people telling me where and when I can smoke. Wish me luck and keep on smoking, if you want to.

Antony Worrall Thompson

My inspiration has always been Jeanne Calment, a Frenchwoman who smoked and drank every day and died a few years ago at the age of 122. When asked the secret of her longevity, she replied: 'I laugh a lot.' Well, you would, wouldn't you?

Victoria Coren

My doctor phoned and said you don't deserve this news, but your lungs are crystal clear.

Chainsmoker Nicky Haslam, at age 63

Smokers of the world unite! We have been bullied and nannied long enough. And if Tony Blair is tempted to follow the lead of Ireland and Italy, let us remind him that only 10.7 million voted Labour last time. But 15 million smoke.

Tom Utley

Smokers pay £19,000 a minute to the Exchequer, and that's enough to pay for the whole police force. Or to put it another way, for every £1 we cost the NHS, we give it £3.60. Please don't encourage the state to dictate how I live my life.

Jeremy Clarkson

The Pipe and Slipper Brigade

I never allow myself to be photographed if I'm not smoking. It's a strict policy I've adhered to for a long time. I initiated it when it became politically correct not to smoke.

> *Maggi Hambling*, on being photographed
> without a cigarette

I know Fabien [Barthez] smokes… In England, it's a rare thing to see a player smoking but, all in all, I prefer that to an alcoholic.

> *Sir Alex Ferguson*

When I smoked myself – up to 60 on some working days – I resolved never to become an anti-smoking bore because I hated them so much. By and large I've stuck to that: if people ask to smoke in our house we gladly cry, 'Yes, of course! Here are ashtrays, cigar clippers, pipe reamers, hookahs, oxygen masks – anything you need!'

> *Simon Hoggart*

Apparently cigarettes contain embalming fluid. This explains why I'm possibly the best-preserved woman in Britain.

> *Sue Carroll*

Smoking, I would now suggest, may be here to stay.

> *James Walton,* editor of The Faber Book of Smoking

The Pipe and Slipper Brigade

I used to smoke all the time but four years ago I changed my smoking habit to smoke only when I'm drinking. However, this policy has had an adverse effect on my drinking habits.

Tommy Walsh

I might smoke more.

Jeremy Irons, announcing his New Year resolution

I enjoy it too much.

David Bowie, explaining why he will never give up smoking

If you want to smoke you should be allowed to do so. For those who smoke it is a natural, relaxing part of life.

Antony Worrall Thompson

When on occasion I'm asked by groups of aspiring writers what they should do to get on, my advice is always, emphatically, smoke. Smoke often and smoke with gusto. It's a little known, indeed little researched, fact of literature and journalism that no non-smoker is worth reading. And writers who give up become crashing bores.

A.A. Gill

The Pipe and Slipper Brigade

Oh, I like smoking, I do. I smoke for my health, my mental health. Tobacco gives you little pauses, a rest from life. I don't suppose anyone smoking a pipe would have road rage, would they?

David Hockney

If I'm seen smoking in the street, people should come up to me and say thank you very much for keeping my tax bill down.

Jeremy Clarkson

I neither coughed nor felt sick. Instead, a sensation of wellbeing filled me, and I became slightly wired, not the reaction you get from alcohol, but sharper and calmer.

John Simpson, experiencing a cigar for the first time

Smoking is, if not my life, then at least my hobby. I love to smoke. Smoking is fun. Smoking is cool. Smoking is, as far as I'm concerned, the entire point of being an adult.

Fran Lebowitz

And a woman is only a woman, but a good cigar is a smoke.

Rudyard Kipling, The Betrothed

It is now proven, beyond a doubt, that smoking is a leading cause of statistics.

Fletcher Knebel

The Pipe and Slipper Brigade

If I cannot smoke in heaven, then I shall not go.

Mark Twain

I want all hellions to quit puffing that hell fume in God's clean air.

Carry Nation

Having smoking and non-smoking sections in the same room is like having urinating and non-urinating sections in a swimming pool.

Ross Parker

I finally quit smoking by using the patch. I put six of them over my mouth.

Wendy Liebman

Giving up smoking is the easiest thing in the world. I know because I've done it thousands of times.

Mark Twain

They say if you smoke you knock off 10 years. But it's the last 10. What do you miss? The drooling years?

John Mendoza

I've been smoking for 30 years now and there's nothing wrong with my lung.

Freddie Starr

Smoking is very bad for you and should only be done because it looks so good. People who don't smoke have a terrible time finding something polite to do with their lips.

P.J. O'Rourke

Pass the Port

DRINK

I have been advised by the best medical authority, at my age, not to attempt to give up alcohol.

W.C. Fields

I love everything that's old – old friends, old times, old manners, old books, old wine.

Oliver Goldsmith, She Stoops to Conquer

I've stopped drinking, but only while I'm asleep.

George Best

A man is a fool if he drinks before he reaches the age of 50, and a fool if he doesn't afterward.

Frank Lloyd Wright

Actually, it only takes one drink to get me loaded. Trouble is, I can't remember if it's the thirteenth or fourteenth.

George Burns

The problem with the world is that everyone is a few drinks behind.

Humphrey Bogart

I exercise strong self-control. I never drink anything stronger than gin before breakfast.

W.C. Fields

You're not drunk if you can lie on the floor without holding on.

Joe E. Lewis

I was in for 10 hours and had 40 pints – beating my previous record by 20 minutes.

George Best, on a blood transfusion for his liver transplant, not on his drinking

Always do sober what you said you'd do drunk. That will teach you to keep your mouth shut.

Ernest Hemingway

Beer is proof that God loves us and wants us to be happy.

Benjamin Franklin

I'm not a heavy drinker; I can sometimes go for hours without touching a drop.

Noel Coward

An alcoholic is anyone you don't like who drinks more than you do.

Dylan Thomas

I know I'm drinking myself to a slow death, but then I'm in no hurry.

Robert Benchley

I often sit back and think, I wish I'd done that and find out later that I already have.

Richard Harris, describing the effects of drinking

I am a drinker with writing problems.

Brendan Behan

I feel sorry for people who don't drink. They wake up in the morning and that's the best they're going to feel all day.

Dean Martin

The difference between a drunk and an alcoholic is that a drunk doesn't have to attend all those meetings.

Arthur Lewis

A tavern is a place where madness is sold by the bottle.

Jonathan Swift

One more drink and I'll be under the host.

Dorothy Parker

The problem with some people is that when they aren't drunk, they're sober.

William Butler Yeats

Beer commercials are so patriotic: 'Made the American Way.' What does that have to do with America? Is that what America stands for? Feeling sluggish and urinating frequently?

Evelyn Waugh

A woman drove me to drink and I didn't even have the decency to thank her.

W.C. Fields

Sometimes when I reflect back on all the beer I drink I feel ashamed. Then I look into the glass and think about the workers in the brewery and all of their hopes and dreams. If I didn't drink this beer, they might be out of work and their dreams would be shattered. Then I say to myself, 'It is better that I drink this beer and let their dreams come true than to be selfish and worry about my liver.'

Jack Handey

I saw a notice that said 'Drink Canada Dry' and I've just started.

Brendan Behan

Pass the Port

I formed a new group called Alcoholics Unanimous. If you don't feel like a drink, you ring another member and he comes over to persuade you.

Richard Harris

Good old days: Beer foamed and drinking water didn't.

Anon

Be wary of strong drink. It can make you shoot at tax collectors… and miss.

Robert A. Heinlein

Milk is for babies. When you grow up you have to drink beer.

Arnold Schwarzenegger

Beer, it's the best damn drink in the world.

Jack Nicholson

I drink too much. The last time I gave a urine sample it had an olive in it.

Rodney Dangerfield

I believe all drunks go to heaven, because they've been through hell on Earth.

Liza Minnelli

When I was a practising alcoholic, I was unbelievable. One side effect was immense suspicion: I'd come off tour like Inspector Clouseau on acid. 'Where's this cornflake come from? It wasn't here before.'

Ozzy Osbourne

When I read about the evils of drinking, I gave up reading.

Henny Youngman

I have a rare intolerance to herbs, which means I can only drink fermented liquids, such as gin.

Julie Walters

Fading Away

MEMORY LOSS

As you get older three things happen. The first is your memory goes, and I can't remember the other two.

Sir Norman Wisdom

I believe the true function of age is memory. I'm recording as fast as I can.

Rita Mae Brown

Fading Away

Just sometimes you bump into people and you think, 'You're my best friend, aren't you? I recognise you. Ooh, you're looking old. What's your name?'

Jenny Eclair, Grumpy Old Women

It's hard to be nostalgic when you can't remember anything.

Anon

Did you ever walk in a room and forget why you walked in? I think that's how dogs spend their lives.

Sue Murphy

Maturity is different from using your ailing health to blackmail your children into doing all your gardening and housework and keeping a diary for comfort and a handy reminder of what you did yesterday.

T. Kinnes

Women over 50 don't have babies because they would put them down and forget where they left them.

Anon

Isn't this amazing? Clinton is getting $8 million for his memoir, Hillary got $8 million for her memoir. That is $16 million for two people who for eight years couldn't remember anything.

Jay Leno

My memory is going. I brush my teeth, and then 10 minutes later I go back and have to feel the toothbrush. Is it wet? Did I just brush them?

Terry Gilliam

I'm suffering from Mallzheimer's disease. I go to the mall and forget where I parked my car.

Anon

I think it would be interesting if old people got anti-Alzheimer's disease where they slowly began to recover other people's lost memories.

George Carlin

Senior Moments

For those of you haven't read the book, it's being published tomorrow.

David Frost

And there's the Victoria Memorial, built as a memorial to Victoria.

David Dimbleby

Richard Burton had a tremendous passion for the English language, especially the spoken and written word.

Frank Bough

It will take time to restore chaos and order.

George W. Bush

Beginning in February 1976 your assistance benefits will be discontinued... Reason: it has been reported to our office that you expired on January 1, 1976.

Excerpt from a letter, Illinois Department of Public Aid

My shoes are size two and a half, the same size as my feet.

Elaine Page

I didn't know *Onward Christian Soldiers* was a Christian song.

Aggie Pate, at a non-denominational mayor's breakfast, Fort Worth, Texas

The Holocaust was an obscene period in our nation's history... this century's history... We all lived in this century. I didn't live in this century.

Dan Quayle

Was it you or your brother who was killed in the war?

Rev. William Spooner

Fiction writing is great. You can make up almost anything.

Ivana Trump, upon finishing her first novel

A bachelor's life is no life for a single man.

Samuel Goldwyn

I love California; I practically grew up in Phoenix.

Dan Quayle

You seem to be a man who likes to keep his feet on the ground – you sail a lot.

Alan Titchmarsh

The Rolling Stones suffered a great loss with the death of Ian Stewart, the man who had for so many years played piano quietly and silently with them on stage.

Andy Peebles

Elderly American lady: 'You speak very good English.'
Me: 'Thank you, but that's because I come from the United Kingdom.'
Elderly American lady: 'Oh, I didn't know they teach English over there.'

Anon

Republicans understand the importance of bondage between a mother and child.

Dan Quayle

Cardial – as in cardial arrest.

Eve Pollard

Senior Moments

Your ambition – is that right – is to abseil across
the English Channel?

Cilla Black

I haven't read any of the autobiographies about
me.

Elizabeth Taylor

The nice thing about being senile is you can hide
your own Easter eggs.

Anon

To see what is in front of one's nose needs a
constant struggle.

George Orwell

I never know how much of what I say is true.

Bette Midler

The future ain't what it used to be.

Yogi Berra

I am wonderful, with a perfect physique, very
charming, rich and look like Jude Law.

Peter Stringfellow

I've always thought that underpopulated countries in Africa are vastly underpolluted.

Lawrence Summers, chief economist of
the World Bank

He hits from both sides of the plate. He's amphibious.

Yogi Berra

One year ago today, the time for excuse-making has come to an end.

George W. Bush

It's always been my dream to come to Madison Square Garden and be the warm-up act for Elvis.

Al Gore

Outside of the killings, Washington has one of the lowest crime rates in the country.

Mayor Marion Barry, Washington, D.C.

I haven't committed a crime. What I did was fail to comply with the law.

David Dinkins, New York City Mayor

And so, in my State of the – my State of the
Union – or state – my speech to the nation,
whatever you want to call it, speech to the nation
– I asked Americans to give 4,000 years – 4,000
hours over the next – the rest of your life – of
service to America. That's what I asked – 4,000
hours.

George W. Bush

Abortion is advocated only by persons who have
themselves been born.

Ronald Reagan

Driving Miss Daisy

I suppose when I am driving, particularly in
London, the thing that makes me angriest is
cyclists, the anarchists of the road... they weave
in and out, ignore the traffic lights and then if
you dare go anywhere near them, they scream at
you like banshees. There's this extraordinary
assumption that we will all have to get out of
their way. But they can do what they damn well
like.

Sheila Hancock, Grumpy Old Women

Regular naps prevent old age, especially if you take them while driving.

Anon

When I am in the car I can have a nice scream because I am contained. I scream very, very loudly, or I scream filthy words and nasty expletives, and nobody can hear.

Michele Hanson, Grumpy Old Women

Have you ever noticed that anybody driving slower than you is an idiot, and anyone going faster than you is a maniac?

George Carlin

If I stop at a zebra crossing, I stop and wave and I'd like them to wave. But if they don't, then I think, 'Well, you bastard, this is the last time I'm gonna do this for you'.

Don Warrington, Grumpy Old Men

Never drive faster than your Guardian Angel can fly.

Anon

Driving Miss Daisy

Apparently more than 80 per cent of open-top sports cars are sold to sad sacks who believe this throbbing mechanical extension makes them look young and virile, not old and desperate.

Amanda Craig

Driving is a spectacular form of amnesia. Everything is to be discovered, everything to be obliterated.

Jean Baudrillard

Drive carefully! Remember, it's not only a car that can be recalled by its maker.

Anon

I drive with my knees. Otherwise, how can I put on my lipstick and talk on my phone?

Sharon Stone

The worst drivers are women in people carriers, men in white vans and anyone in a baseball cap. That's just about everyone.

Paul O'Grady

You know, somebody actually complimented me on my driving today. They left a little note on the windscreen; it said 'Parking Fine.'

Tommy Cooper

As a senior citizen was driving down the freeway, his car phone rang. Answering, he heard his wife's voice urgently warning him, 'Henry, I just heard on the news that there's a car going the wrong way on 280. Please be careful!' Henry said, 'Hell, it's not just one car. It's hundreds of them!'

Anon

I hate driving more than anything in the whole world. I'm just an awful, awful driver. I get lost, I hit things: parked cars, one moving car, a pole in my parking garage. Just when I think I got everything under control, I'll miss seeing something out of the corner of my mirror.

Rachel Leigh

Sure, I've gotten old. I've had two bypass surgeries, a hip replacement, new knees... I've fought prostate cancer and diabetes. I'm half blind, can't hear anything quieter than a jet engine, and take 40 different medications that make me dizzy, winded and subject to blackouts. I have bouts with dementia, poor circulation, hardly feel my hands or feet any more, can't remember if I'm 85 or 92, but... thank God, I still have my Florida driver's licence.

Anon

The best car safety device is a rear-view mirror with a cop in it.

Dudley Moore

Pounds, shillings and pence

If you stay in Beverly Hills too long you become a Mercedes.

Robert Redford

Pounds, shillings and pence

Money isn't everything, but it sure keeps you in touch with your children.

J. Paul Getty

I've got all the money I'll ever need if I die by four o'clock this afternoon.

Henny Youngman

Money is something you have to make in case you don't die.

Max Asnas

I'm living so far beyond my income that we may almost be said to be living apart.

e.e. cummings

There's no reason to be the richest man in the cemetery. You can't do any business from there.

Colonel Sanders

Another good thing about being poor is that when you are 70 your children will not have declared you legally insane in order to gain control of your estate.

Woody Allen

Most men love money and security more, and creation and construction less, as they get older.

John Maynard Keynes

Parents should be given only a modest and sensible allowance. And they should be encouraged to save up for things. This builds character. It also helps pay for the funeral.

P.J. O'Rourke

Vintage Vigour

I don't exercise. If God wanted me to bend over, he'd have put diamonds on the floor.

Joan Rivers

I get my exercise running to the funerals of my friends who exercise.

Barry Gray

I consider exercise vulgar. It makes people smell.

Alec Yuill Thornton

Vintage Vigour

To resist the frigidity of old age, one must combine the body, the mind, and the heart. And to keep these in parallel vigour one must exercise, study, and love.

Alan Bleasdale

Once I realised how expensive funerals are, I began to exercise and watch my diet.

Thomas Sowell

If God wanted me to touch my toes, he would have put them on my knees.

Roseanne Barr

I get my exercise acting as a pallbearer to my friends who exercise.

Chauncey Depew

Exercise is bunk. If you are healthy you don't need it. If you are sick you shouldn't take it.

Henry Ford

I like long walks, especially when they are taken by people who annoy me.

Fred Allen

My idea of exercise is a good brisk sit down.

Phyllis Diller

Jogging is very beneficial. It's good for your legs and your feet. It's also very good for the ground. It makes it feel needed.

Charles M. Schulz

Jogging is for people who aren't intelligent enough to watch television.

Victoria Wood

In the gym, I only wear black and diamonds.

Donatella Versace

You know you're into middle age when first you realise that caution is the only thing you care to exercise.

Charles Ghigna

The trouble with jogging is that by the time you realise you're not in shape for it, it's too far to walk back.

Franklin P. Jones

I often take exercise. Only yesterday I had breakfast in bed.

Oscar Wilde

I bought all those celebrity exercise videos. I love to sit and eat cookies and watch them.

Dolly Parton

Vintage Vigour

I have a punishing workout regimen. Every day I do three minutes on a treadmill, then I lie down, drink a glass of vodka and smoke a cigarette.

Anthony Hopkins

I've exercised with women so thin that buzzards followed them to their cars.

Erma Bombeck

I diet every day of my life. After 40 you've got to.

Kim Cattrall

Passing the vodka bottle. And playing the guitar.

Keith Richards, on how he keeps fit

I do try and keep fit, but it's a half-hearted battle. I'll go for a jog once a fortnight and then feel ill for two days afterwards. And now and again I'll join a health club, but the trauma of filling in the form and having my photo taken for the membership card usually puts me off going for about 12 months. But I'm still optimistic that one day I'll be offered a guest role in *Baywatch*.

Steve Coogan

The first time I see a jogger smiling, I'll consider it.

Joan Rivers

Sometimes I run around Regent's Park and go to the gym, I can manage about an hour, but stop for a cigarette every so often.

Julian Clary

You know you've reached middle age when your weightlifting consists of merely standing up.

Bob Hope

A Quiet Five Minutes

THE AFTERNOON NAP

I'll sleep when I'm dead.

Warren Zevon

Sleep – those little slices of death, how I loathe them.

Edgar Allan Poe

No day is so bad it can't be fixed with a nap.

Carrie Snow

Two things I dislike about my granddaughter – when she won't take her afternoon nap, and when she won't let me take mine.

Gene Perret

I usually take a two-hour nap from one to four.

Yogi Berra

A Quiet Five Minutes

A man of 60 has spent 20 years in bed and over three years in eating.

Arnold Bennett

Set aside half an hour every day to do all your worrying, then take a nap during this period.

Anon

I never take a nap after dinner but when I have had a bad night; and then the nap takes me.

Samuel Johnson

There is more refreshment and stimulation in a nap, even of the briefest, than in all the alcohol ever distilled.

Ovid

A nap, my friend, is a brief period of sleep which overtakes superannuated persons when they endeavour to entertain unwelcome visitors or to listen to scientific lectures.

George Bernard Shaw

I catnap now and then, but I think while I nap, so it's not a waste of time.

Martha Stewart

60! Now is the time to make your mark on the world – explore the Antarctic or become an

astronaut. Make your mind up to take on
exciting new challenges – straight after your
afternoon nap.

Anon

Every businessman over 50 should have a daily nap
and nip; a short nap after lunch and a relaxing
highball before dinner.

Dr. Sara Murray Jordan

I have left orders to be awakened at any time in case
of national emergency, even if I'm in a cabinet
meeting.

Ronald Reagan

Menopausal Moments

YOU KNOW YOU'RE MENOPAUSAL WHEN…

…you're adding chocolate chips to your cheese
omelette.

…the dryer has shrunk every last pair of your jeans.

…everyone around you has an attitude problem.

…your husband is suddenly agreeing to everything
you say.

Menopausal Moments

…you're using your cellular phone to dial up every bumper sticker that says 'How's my driving – call 1–800–***–.'

…everyone's head looks like an invitation to batting practice.

…you're convinced there's a God and he's male.

…you can't believe they don't make a tampon bigger than Super Plus.

…you're sure that everyone is scheming to drive you crazy.

…the ibuprofen bottle is empty and you bought it yesterday.

All Anonymous

Male menopause is a lot more fun than female menopause. With female menopause you gain weight and get hot flashes. Male menopause – you get to date young girls and drive motorcycles.

Rita Rudner

I do get hot. Sometimes I think, 'Oh I can smell the menopause on me.' You know, it's kind of BO and Prozac and furniture polish.

Jenny Eclair, Grumpy Old Women

My first day as a woman and I am already having hot flushes.

Robin Williams, Mrs. Doubtfire

Middle-aged men are fine if they accept that they're middle-aged men. In fact, they're rather interesting when they accept that they're middle-aged men. But when they decide that they're going to act as if they're 19 or 20, and dress in a style that is inappropriate to that age, then it really is pathetic.

Ann Widdecombe, Grumpy Old Women

Rock and menopause do not mix. It is not good, it sucks and every day I fight it to the death, or, at the very least, not let it take me over.

Stevie Nicks

Charlotte: Listen to this: sometime in the ten years before menopause, you may experience symptoms including all-month-long PMS, fluid retention, insomnia, depression, hot flashes or irregular periods.
Carrie: On the plus side, people start to give up their seats for you on the bus.

Sex and the City

Inevitably I'm being given a hard time for being a typical ageing male, going off and packing in the wife.

Rick Stein

The Cracks of Time

For my sister's fiftieth birthday, I sent her a singing mammogram.

Steven Wright

I'm out of oestrogen and I've got a gun!

Bumper Sticker

The seven dwarves of menopause; itchy, bitchy, sweaty, sleepy, bloated, forgetful and psycho.

Anon

I'm developing a new fondness for Michael Douglas, now that he's getting all menopausal and wrinkly.

John Patterson

I certainly hope I'm not still answering child-star questions by the time I reach menopause.

Christina Ricci

The Cracks of Time

FADING LOOKS

How pleasant is the day when we give up striving to be young – or slender.

William James

Most women are not as young as they are painted.

Max Beerbohm

My face looks like a wedding cake left out in the rain.

W.H. Auden

As we get older, our bodies get shorter and our anecdotes get longer.

Robert Quillen

I guess I look like a rock quarry that someone has dynamited.

Charles Bronson

Like a lot of fellows around here, I have a furniture problem. My chest has fallen into my drawers.

Billy Casper

If a woman tells you she's 20 and looks 16, she's 12. If she tells you she's 26 and looks 26, she's damn near 40.

Chris Rock

Robert Redford used to be such a handsome man and now look at him: everything has dropped, expanded and turned a funny colour.

George Best

The Cracks of Time

The outer passes away; the innermost is the same yesterday, today, and forever.

Thomas Carlyle

Many of my contemporaries have terrible feet, deformed by bunions, permanent corns and layers of dead skin like rock strata.

Sue Townsend

The problem with beauty is that it's like being born rich and getting poorer.

Joan Collins

Time may be a great healer, but it's a lousy beautician.

Lucille S. Harper

I ain't what I used to be, but who the hell is?

Dizzy Dean

I spent seven hours in a beauty shop – and that was just for the estimate.

Phyllis Diller

Take my photograph? You might as well use a picture of a relief map of Ireland!

Nancy Astor

I have a face like the behind of an elephant.

Charles Laughton

Naked, I had a body that invited burial.

Spike Milligan

One day you look in the mirror and you realise that the face you are shaving is your father's.

Robert Harris

Some people, no matter how old they get, never lose their beauty – they merely move it from their faces into their hearts.

Martin Buxbaum

When I look in the mirror I don't see a rock star any more. I see a little balding old guy who looks like someone's uncle.

Pete Townshend

Wrinkles should merely indicate where smiles have been.

Mark Twain

You know you're getting fat when you can pinch an inch on your forehead.

John Mendoza

People say that age is just a state of mind. I say it's more about the state of your body.

Geoffrey Parfitt

The Cracks of Time

Time wounds all heels.

Groucho Marx

I have a face that is a cross between two pounds of halibut and an explosion in an old clothes closet.

David Niven

I look just like the girl next door... if you happen to live next to an amusement park.

Dolly Parton

Old age is when the liver spots show through your gloves.

Phyllis Diller

A man's as old as he's feeling. A woman as old as she looks.

Mortimer Collins

The excesses of our youth are cheques written against our age and they are payable with interest 30 years later.

Charles Caleb Colton

Looking 50 is great – if you're 60.

Joan Rivers

At age 50, everyone has the face he deserves.

George Orwell

The Cracks of Time

At 50, you have the choice of keeping your face or your figure and it's much better to keep your face.

Barbara Cartland

Anatomically speaking, a bust is here today and gone tomorrow.

Isobel Barnett

He must have had a magnificent build before his stomach went in for a career of its own.

Margaret Halsey

Muscles come and go; flab lasts.

Bill Vaughan

You can only perceive real beauty in a person as they get older.

Anouk Aimée

Men become much more attractive when they start looking older. But it doesn't do much for women, though we do have an advantage: make-up.

Bette Davis

Intellectual blemishes, like facial ones, grow more prominent with age.

François de La Rochefoucauld

The Cracks of Time

I'd like to change my butt. It hangs a little too long.
God forbid what it will look like when I'm older.
It will probably be dragging along on the ground
behind me.

Teri Hatcher

I'm tired of all this nonsense about beauty being
only skin-deep. That's deep enough. What do you
want – an adorable pancreas?

Jean Kerr

I don't believe make-up and the right hairstyle
alone can make a woman beautiful. The most
radiant woman in the room is the one full of life
and experience.

Sharon Stone

If you want to look young and thin, hang around
old fat people.

Jim Eason

Thank God for beauty products because at least
they give you hope. Even if they do nothing for
you, you can sort of slam the box to your forehead
and think it's helping. And it has to be expensive
stuff because if it's cheap stuff, it won't work. I'm
not interested in cheap stuff. I don't care if it's all
packaging, that's fine by me. Just as long as it sells
me a dream.

Nina Myskow, Grumpy Old Women

It's time we stopped worrying about losing our looks and started celebrating the gifts of age: I feel yummier than ever.

Sela Ward

I am sitting here thinking how nice it is that wrinkles don't hurt.

Anon

I don't think age is an ugly process. I think age is a beautiful thing. I love wrinkles. I don't like falling down. If I just wrinkle, I may not touch. If I fall down, I'll lift up.

Linda Evangelista

A beautiful lady is an accident of nature. A beautiful old lady is a work of art.

Louis Nizer

When you have loved as she has loved, you grow old beautifully.

W. Somerset Maugham

Midlife has hit you when you stand naked in front of a mirror and can see your rear end without turning around!

Anon

The older I get, the more I feel almost beautiful.

Sharon Olds

The Cracks of Time

I guess I don't so much mind being old, as I mind being fat and old.

Peter Gabriel

You can take no credit for beauty at 16. But if you are beautiful at 60, it will be your own soul's doing.

Marie Stopes

It really costs me a lot emotionally to watch myself on-screen. I think of myself, and feel like I'm quite young, and then I look at this old man with the baggy chins and the tired eyes and the receding hairline and all that.

Gene Hackman

Midlife is when the growth of the hair on our legs slows down. This gives us plenty of time to care for our newly acquired moustache.

Anon

Middle age is when your wife tells you to pull in your stomach, and you already have.

Jack Barry

I am going to carry on colouring my hair, wearing diamonds and painting my nails until the day I die.

Jenni Murray

Liza Minnelli looks like a very old 13.

Jonathan Ross

Midlife women no longer have upper arms, we have wingspans. We are no longer women in sleeveless shirts; we are flying squirrels in drag.

Anon

I think that the longer I look good, the better gay men feel.

Cher

It's okay to be fat. So you're fat. Just be fat and shut up about it.

Roseanne Barr

It's simple, if it jiggles it's fat.

Arnold Schwarzenegger

The older you get, the tougher it is to lose weight, because by then your body and your fat are really good friends.

Anon

If I had been around when Rubens was painting, I would have been revered as a fabulous model. Kate Moss? Well, she would have been the paintbrush.

Dawn French

The Cracks of Time

I'm going to have wrinkles really soon.

Cher

Character contributes to beauty. It fortifies a
woman as her youth fades.

Jacqueline Bisset

In middle life, the human back is spoiling for a
technical knockout and will use the flimsiest
excuse, even a sneeze, to fall apart.

Elwyn Brooks White

Brilliantly lit from stem to stern, she looked like a
sagging birthday cake.

Walter Lord

Even with all my wrinkles! I am beautiful!

Edward Everett Hale

Wear a smile and have friends; wear a scowl and
have wrinkles.

George Eliot

Well, her face was so wrinkled it looked like seven
miles of bad road.

W.C. Fields

Folding Back the Years

COSMETIC SURGERY

I want to grow old without facelifts. I want to have the courage to be loyal to the face I have made.

Marilyn Monroe

I'd make plastic surgery compulsory for every woman over 40.

Simon Cowell

My husband said 'show me your boobs' and I had to pull up my skirt… so it was time to get them done!

Dolly Parton

Please don't retouch my wrinkles. It took me so long to earn them.

Anna Magnani

A plastic surgeon's office is the only place where no one gets offended when you pick your nose.

MAD Magazine

I don't suggest that her face has been lifted, but there's a possibility that her body has been lowered.

Clive James

Folding Back the Years

The only parts left of my original body are my elbows.

Phyllis Diller

Look at Cher. One more face lift and she'll be wearing a beard.

Jennifer Saunders

Sylvester Stallone's mother's plastic surgery looks so bad it could have been bought through a mail order catalogue.

Graham Norton

I don't need plastic surgery. I need Lourdes.

Paul O'Grady

Why fear terrorists? With treatments like botox, women are waging germ warfare on themselves at £250 a pop.

Kathy Lette

If anybody says their facelift doesn't hurt, they're lying. It was like I'd spent the night with an axe murderer.

Sharon Osbourne

I was going to have cosmetic surgery until I noticed that the doctor's office was full of portraits by Picasso.

Rita Rudner

My Aching Bones!

HEALTH

First the doctor told me the good news: I was
going to have a disease named after me.

Steve Martin

My father died of cancer when I was a teenager.
He had it before it became popular.

Goodman Ace

You know you're getting old when everything
hurts. And what doesn't hurt doesn't work.

Hy Gardner

The trouble with heart disease is that the first
symptom is often hard to deal with – sudden
death.

Michael Phelps

I am afraid… that health begins, after 70, and often
long before, to have a meaning different from that
which it had at 30. But it is culpable to murmur at
the established order of the creation, as it is vain to
oppose it. He that lives, must grow old; and he that
would rather grow old than die, has God to thank
for the infirmities of old age.

Samuel Johnson

My Aching Bones!

My doctor gave me six months to live, but when I couldn't pay the bill he gave me six more.

Walter Matthau

Life begins at 40 – but so do fallen arches, rheumatism, faulty eyesight, and the tendency to tell a story to the same person, three or four times.

William Feather

As the arteries grow hard, the heart grows soft.

Henry Louis Mencken

Nobody expects to trust his body overmuch after the age of 50.

Edward Hoagland

The trouble about always trying to preserve the health of the body is that it is so difficult to do without destroying the health of the mind.

G.K. Chesterton

Two elderly gentlemen from a retirement centre were sitting on a bench under a tree when one turned to the other and said, 'Ted, I'm 83 years old now and I'm just full of aches and pains. I know you're about my age. How do you feel?'

Ted said, 'I feel like a newborn baby.'

'Really? Like a newborn baby?'

'Yep. No hair, no teeth, and I think I just wet my pants.'

Anon

I drive way too fast to worry about cholesterol.

Steven Wright

We all get heavier as we get older because there is a lot more information in our heads.

Vlade Divac

The spiritual eyesight improves as the physical eyesight declines.

Plato

Don't you think it's unnerving that doctors call what they do 'Practice'?

George Carlin

Quit worrying about your health. It'll go away.

Robert Orben

Each year it grows harder to make ends meet – the ends I refer to are hands and feet.

Richard Armour

It's no longer a question of staying healthy. It's a question of finding a sickness you like.

Jackie Mason

My Aching Bones!

A woman walked up to a little old man rocking in a chair on his porch.

'I couldn't help noticing how happy you look,' she said. 'What's your secret for a long happy life?'

'I smoke three packs of cigarettes a day,' he said. 'I also drink a case of whisky a week, eat fatty foods, and never exercise.'

'That's amazing,' the woman said. 'How old are you?'

'26,' he said.

Anon

Never under any circumstances take a sleeping pill and a laxative on the same night.

Dave Barry

So who's perfect? Washington had false teeth. Franklin was nearsighted. Mussolini had syphilis. Unpleasant things have been said about Walt Whitman and Oscar Wilde. Tchaikovsky had his problems, too. And Lincoln was constipated.

John O'Hara

I have finally come to the conclusion that a good reliable set of bowels is worth more to man than any quantity of brains.

Josh Billings

My grandfather is hard of hearing. He needs to read lips. I don't mind him reading lips, but he uses one of those yellow highlighters.

Brian Kiley

A man does not die of love or his liver or even of old age; he dies of being a man.

Percival Arland Ussher

I think most people would pick sudden heart attack and in sleep. We assume that's the best way to die, because you never know.

Jack Kevorkian

There are only three things that can kill a farmer: lightning, rolling over in a tractor, and old age.

Bill Bryson

For years I was an undiagnosed anorexic, suffering from a little-known variant of the disease, where, freakishly, the appetite turns in on itself and demands more and more food, forcing the sufferer to gain several stones in weight and wear men's V-necked pullovers. My condition has stabilised now, but I can never stray too far from cocoa-based products and I keep a small cracknel-type candy in my brassiere at all times. Fortunately, I wear a 'D' cup so there is plenty of room for sweetmeats...

Victoria Wood

Doctor, Doctor

I feel stronger, but physically I feel like I'm falling apart. Every day I get a new pain or ache and think, 'Oh, that will be a hip replacement in a couple of years!'

Yasmin Le Bon

Money cannot buy health, but I'd settle for a diamond-studded wheelchair.

Dorothy Parker

I think that in youth you never view an ailment as possibly fatal. When you get an ailment in middle age, you are automatically planning your own funeral…

Will Self

I have such poor vision I can date anybody.

Garry Shandling

Doctor, Doctor

THE MEDICAL PROFESSION

In the name of Hippocrates, doctors have invented the most exquisite form of torture ever known to man: survival.

Luis Buñuel

Cured yesterday of my disease, I died last night of my physician.

Matthew Prior

The medics can now stretch life out an additional dozen years but they don't tell you that most of these years are going to be spent flat on your back while some ghoul with thick glasses and a matted skull peers at you through a machine that's hot out of 'Space Patrol'.

Groucho Marx

Beware of the young doctor and the old barber.

Benjamin Franklin

The doctor called Mrs. Cohen saying, 'Mrs. Cohen, your cheque came back.' Mrs. Cohen answered, 'So did my arthritis!' The doctor says, 'You'll live to be 60!' 'I AM 60!' 'See, what did I tell you?'

Henny Youngman

Too many good docs are getting out of the business. Too many OB-GYNs aren't able to practise their love with women all across this country.

George W. Bush

My doctor is wonderful. Once, in 1955, when I couldn't afford an operation, he touched up the X-rays.

Joey Bishop

Doctor, Doctor

After two days in hospital, I took a turn for the nurse.

W.C. Fields

Doctors are the same as lawyers; the only difference is that lawyers merely rob you, whereas doctors rob you and kill you too.

Anton Chekhov

One of the most difficult things to contend with in a hospital is that assumption on the part of the staff that because you have lost your gall bladder you have also lost your mind.

Jean Kerr

Keep away from physicians. It is all probing and guessing and pretending with them. They leave it to Nature to cure in her own time, but they take the credit. As well as very fat fees.

Anthony Burgess

My doctor tells me I'm in very good nick. The most positive way to think about death is to try to live.

Michael Caine

The ultimate indignity is to be given a bedpan by a stranger who calls you by your first name.

Maggie Kuhn

I'm not feeling very well, I need a doctor immediately. Ring the nearest golf course.

Groucho Marx

Thanks to modern medicine we are no longer forced to endure prolonged pain, disease, discomfort and wealth.

Robert Orben

At my age, every doctor says the same thing; it's either something I have to live with – or something I have to live without.

Anon

Never go to a doctor whose office plants have died.

Erma Bombeck

My doctor gave me two weeks to live. I hope they are in August.

Ronnie Shakes

Our doctor would never really operate unless it was necessary. He was just that way. If he didn't need the money, he wouldn't lay a hand on you.

Herb Shriner

My doctor once said to me, 'Do you think I'm here for the good of your health?'

Bob Monkhouse

America's health care system is second only to
Japan... Canada, Sweden, Great Britain... well, all
of Europe. But you can thank your lucky stars we
don't live in Paraguay!

Homer Simpson

A hospital bed is a parked taxi, with the meter
running.

Groucho Marx

A woman tells her doctor, 'I've got a bad back.' The
doctor says, 'It's old age.' The woman says, 'I want a
second opinion.' The doctor says: 'Okay - you're
ugly as well.'

Tommy Cooper

My kid could get a bad X-ray and I could get a call
from the doctor saying I have something growing
in my bum and that would change my perspective
on everything instantaneously, on what is and what
is not important.

Tom Hanks

I've wrestled with reality for 35 years, and I'm
happy, Doctor, I finally won out over it.

Jimmy Stewart, Harvey

Dick Cheney said he was running again. He said
his health was fine, 'I've got a doctor with me 24

hours a day.' Yeah, that's always the sign of a man in good health, isn't it?

David Letterman

I kept thinking about that large doctor, sweaty, who brought my mother home after the first heart attack. He said, 'Don't ever get angry at your mother, that might kill her.' That set off my demons, I think.

Gene Wilder

I told the doctor I broke my leg in two places. He told me to quit going to those places.

Henny Youngman

Dad always thought laughter was the best medicine, which I guess is why several of us died of tuberculosis.

Jack Handey

I don't know why people question the academic training of an athlete. 50 per cent of the doctors in this country graduated in the bottom half of their classes.

Al McGuire

When I go in for a physical, they no longer ask how old I am. They just carbon-date me.

Ronald Reagan

You Know You're Getting Old When...

There's a new medical crisis. Doctors are reporting that many men are having allergic reactions to latex condoms. They say they cause severe swelling. So what's the problem?

Dustin Hoffman

I know of nothing more laughable than a doctor who does not die of old age.

Voltaire

On a Friday night it's like a field hospital in the Battle of the Somme. There's blokes with blood coming out of their heads and Bacardi Breezer bottles stuck in their necks.

John O'Farrell, on A&E departments in Grumpy Old Men

You Know You're Getting Old When...

...the only thing you want for your birthday is not to be reminded of it.

...'Happy Hour' turns out to be a nap!

...it takes you all night to do what you used to do all night!

You Know You're Getting Old When...

...you sink your teeth into an apple and they stay there!

...your back goes out more often than you do!

...you can't get your rocking chair started!

...it feels like the morning after and you haven't been anywhere.

...you get winded playing chess.

...being a little hippie does not have the same meaning as it did in the 60s.

...everything either dries up or leaks.

...you go for a mammogram and you realise it is the only time someone will ever ask you to appear topless in a film.

...your wife gives up sex for Lent, and you don't know till the 4th of July.

All Anonymous

...you've lost all your marvels.

Merry Browne

...you walk into a record store and everything you like has been marked down to $1.99.

Jack Simmons

…All the names in your black book have M.D. after them.

Arnold Palmer

…The candles cost more than the cake.

George Burns

The Good Old Days

MEMORIES

Nothing is more responsible for the good old days than a bad memory.

Franklin P. Adams

When I was young I was called a rugged individualist. When I was in my 50s I was considered eccentric. Here I am doing and saying the same things I did then and I'm labelled senile.

George Burns

We have all passed a lot of water since then.

Samuel Goldwyn

The one thing I remember about Christmas was that my father used to take me out in a boat about 10 miles offshore on Christmas Day, and I used to have to swim back. Extraordinary. It was a ritual.

Mind you, that wasn't the hard part. The difficult bit was getting out of the sack.

John Cleese

When you finally go back to your old home town, you find it wasn't the old home you missed but your childhood.

Sam Ewing

The older you get, the more you tell it like it used to be.

Anon

When I was a boy, the Dead Sea was only sick.

George Burns

When I was a kid my parents moved a lot, but I always found them.

Rodney Dangerfield

I was so naive as a kid I used to sneak behind the barn and do nothing.

Johnny Carson

Most people like the old days best – they were younger then.

Anon

I can remember when the air was clean and sex was dirty.

George Burns

The Good Old Days

There's a lot to do when you're a kid – spiders to catch, girls to poke in the eye – stuff to be getting on with.

Alan Davies

I remember when I was seven, sitting backstage in Vegas while these topless showgirls adjusted their G-strings in front of me. It was a strange way to grow up.

Donny Osmond

Nostalgia, the vice of the aged. We watch so many old movies our memories come in monochrome.

Angela Carter

The older a man gets, the farther he had to walk to school as a boy.

Anon

In every age 'the good old days' were a myth. No one ever thought they were good at the time. For every age has consisted of crises that seemed intolerable to the people who lived through them.

Brooks Atkinson

Nostalgia is a file that removes the rough edges from the good old days.

Doug Larson

We seem to be going through a period of nostalgia, and everyone seems to think yesterday was better than today. I don't think it was, and I would advise you not to wait 10 years before admitting today was great. If you're hung up on nostalgia, pretend today is yesterday and just go out and have one hell of a time

Art Buchwald

You don't appreciate a lot of stuff in school until you get older. Little things like being spanked every day by a middle-aged woman: stuff you pay good money for in later life.

Emo Philips

What's in An Age?

It is so comic to hear oneself called old, even at 90, I suppose!

Alice James

Age puzzles me. I thought it was a quiet time. My 70s were interesting and fairly serene, but my 80s are passionate. I grow more intense as I age.

Florida Scott-Maxwell

The hardest years in life are those between 10 and 70.

Helen Hayes

What's in An Age?

There's one advantage to being 102. No peer pressure.

Dennis Wolfberg

People under 24 think old age starts around 55, those over 75, on the other hand, believe that youth doesn't end until the age of 58.

Alexander Chancellor

I'm 65 and I guess that puts me in with the geriatrics. But if there were 15 months in every year, I'd only be 48. That's the trouble with us. We number everything. Take women, for example. I think they deserve to have more than 12 years between the ages of 28 and 40.

James Thurber

No one is so old as to think he cannot live one more year.

Marcus T. Cicero

No woman should ever be quite accurate about her age. It looks so calculating.

Oscar Wilde

Who wants to be 95? 94-year-olds.

George Burns

The age of a woman doesn't mean a thing. The best tunes are played on the oldest fiddles.

Ralph Waldo Emerson

Autumn is really the best of seasons; and I'm not sure that old age isn't the best part of life.

C.S. Lewis

I'm not interested in age. People who tell me their age are silly. You're as old as you feel.

Elizabeth Arden

Like many women my age, I am 28 years old.

Mary Schmitt

The seven ages of man: spills, drills, thrills, bills, ills, pills and wills.

Richard John Needham

How the hell should I know? Most of the people my age are dead.

Casey Stengel, on the subject of his age

Age ain't nothin' but a number. But age is other things too. It is wisdom, if one has lived one's life properly. It is experience and knowledge. And it is getting to know all the ways the world turns, so that if you cannot turn the world the way you want, you can at least get out of the way so you won't get run over.

Miriam Makeba

A sexagenarian? At his age? I think that's disgusting.

Gracie Allen

What's in An Age?

You can judge your age by the amount of pain you feel when you come in contact with a new idea.

John Nuveen

I do wish I could tell you my age but it's impossible. It keeps changing all the time.

Greer Garson

I am luminous with age.

Meridel Le Sueur

Age is not measured by years. Nature does not equally distribute energy. Some people are born old and tired while others are going strong at 70.

Dorothy Thompson

Your 50s are mature, reliable and dependable – or boring, predictable and conventional.

T. Kinnes

Old age is a special problem for me because I've never been able to shed the mental image I have of myself – a lad of about 19.

E.B. White

I'm 57. I can't look like a 30-year-old. You try to hold age at bay, but there comes a point when you just have to give up gracefully.

Elton John

What's in An Age?

The biggest disadvantage of old age is that you can't outgrow it.

Anon

Old age brings along with its uglinesses the comfort that you will soon be out of it – which ought to be a substantial relief to such discontented pendulums as we are.

Ralph Waldo Emerson

You can calculate Zsa Zsa Gabor's age by the rings on her fingers.

Bob Hope

At 65 and drawing a state pension, I was delighted to discover that only people under 45 would regard me as old, even though sadly nobody would actually call me young.

Alexander Chancellor

Nobody knows the age of the human race, but everybody agrees that it is old enough to know better.

Anon

Age is whatever you think it is. You are as old as you think you are.

Muhammad Ali

Writing the Memoirs

When you get to my age you either run away or jump in with both feet.

Jan Leeming

I think all this talk about age is foolish. Every time I'm one year older, everyone else is too.

Gloria Swanson

Age is not a handicap. Age is nothing but a number. It is how you use it.

Diesel Payne

Nobody grows old by merely living a number of years. People grow old only by deserting their ideals. Years wrinkle the face, but to give up enthusiasm wrinkles the soul.

Anon

Age is just a number. It's totally irrelevant unless, of course, you happen to be a bottle of wine.

Joan Collins

Writing the Memoirs

Keep a diary, and someday it'll keep you.

Mae West

Writing the Memoirs

I was born because it was a habit in those days, people didn't know anything else.

Will Rogers

My father had a profound influence on me, he was a lunatic.

Spike Milligan

I used to think I was an interesting person, but I must tell you how sobering a thought it is to realise your life's story fills about 35 pages and you have, actually, not much to say.

Roseanne Barr

I wanted to be president of the United States. I really did. The older I get, the less preposterous the idea seems.

Alec Baldwin

Thank goodness I was never sent to school: it would have rubbed off some of the originality.

Beatrix Potter

I succeeded by saying what everyone else is thinking.

Joan Rivers

I wrote the story myself. It's about a girl who lost her reputation and never missed it.

Mae West

Writing the Memoirs

Each has his past shut in him like the leaves of a book known to him by his heart, and his friends can only read the title.

Virginia Woolf

When I was growing up, there were two things that were unpopular in my house. One was me, and the other was my guitar.

Bruce Springsteen

I wasn't as smart then as I am now. But who ever is?

Tina Turner

When I realised what I had turned out to be was a lousy, two-bit pool hustler and a drunk, I wasn't depressed at all. I was glad to have a profession.

Danny McGoorty, Irish pool player

In my 20s, my pleasures tended to be physical. In my 30s, my pleasures tended to be intellectual. I can't say which was more exquisite.

Steve Kangas

I always wanted to be an explorer, but – it seemed I was doomed to be nothing more than a very silly person.

Michael Palin

Writing the Memoirs

I have never described the time I was in *Doctor Who*
as anything except a kind of ecstatic success, but all
the rest has been rather a muddle and a
disappointment. Compared to *Doctor Who*, it has
been an outrageous failure really — it's so boring.

Tom Baker

I'm writing an unauthorized autobiography.

Steven Wright

I don't think anyone should write his autobiography
until after he's dead.

Samuel Goldwyn

An autobiography is an obituary in serial form
with the last instalment missing.

Quentin Crisp

Rebecca was a busy liar in her distinguished old
age, reinventing her past for gullible biographers.

Walter Clemons, on Rebecca West

All I ever seemed to get was the kind of girl who
had a special dispensation from Rome to wear the
thickest part of her legs below the knee.

Hugh Leonard

I couldn't wait for success, so I went on ahead
without it.

Jonathan Winters

Writing the Memoirs

I spent 90 per cent of my money on women and drink. The rest I wasted.

George Best

On what?

> *Chris Eubank*, when asked if he had ever thought
> of writing an autobiography

I always knew looking back on my tears would bring me laughter, but I never knew looking back on my laughter would make me cry.

Cat Stevens

Forty pictures I was in, and all I remember is 'What kind of bra will you be wearing today, honey?' That was always the area of big decision – from the neck to the navel.

Donna Reed

The really good idea is always traceable back quite a long way, often to a not very good idea which sparked off another idea that was only slightly better, which somebody else misunderstood in such a way that they then said something which was really rather interesting.

John Cleese

My toughest fight was with my first wife, and she won every round.

Muhammad Ali

It was no great tragedy being Judy Garland's daughter. I had tremendously interesting childhood years – except they had little to do with being a child.

Liza Minnelli

This is the second most bizarre thing ever to happen to me. The first was when I was sued by a woman who claimed she became pregnant because she watched me on TV and I bent her contraceptive coil.

Uri Geller

This bikini made me a success.

Ursula Andress

I wanted revenge; I wanted to dance on the graves of a few people who made me unhappy. It's a pretty infantile way to go through life – I'll show them – but I've done it, and I've got more than I ever dreamed of.

Anthony Hopkins

I sold the memoirs of my sex life to a publisher – they are going to make a board game out of it.

Woody Allen

I grew up in Europe, where the history comes from.

Eddie Izzard

Writing the Memoirs

I was coming home from kindergarten – well, they told me it was kindergarten. I found out later I had been working in a factory for ten years. It's good for a kid to know how to make gloves.

Ellen DeGeneres

Success didn't spoil me, I've always been insufferable.

Fran Lebowitz

My childhood was a period of waiting for the moment when I could send everyone and everything connected with it to hell.

Igor Stravinsky

I can't understand why I flunked American history. When I was a kid there was so little of it.

George Burns

There is nothing that makes you so aware of the improvisation of human existence as a song unfinished or an old address book.

Carson McCullers

I didn't really say everything I said.

Yogi Berra

It took me 15 years to discover I had no talent for writing, but I couldn't give it up, because by that time I was too famous.

Robert Benchley

History will be kind to me for I intend to write it.

Winston Churchill

There used to be a real me, but I had it surgically removed.

Peter Sellers

Acting is merely the art of keeping a large group of people from coughing.

Sir Ralph Richardson

As a kid, I knew I wanted to be either a cartoonist or an astronaut. The latter was never much of a possibility, as I don't even like riding in elevators.

Bill Watterson

The most important thing I would learn in school was that almost everything I would learn in school would be utterly useless. When I was 15 I knew the principal industries of the Ruhr Valley, the underlying causes of World War One and what Peig Sayers had for her dinner every day… What I wanted to know when I was 15 was the best way to chat up girls. That is what I still want to know.

Joseph O'Connor, The Secret World of the Irish Male

If I'd only known, I would have been a locksmith.

Albert Einstein

The Trouble Today is...

We live in an age when pizza gets to your home before the police.

Jeff Marder

Everything is drive-through. In California, they even have a burial service called Jump-In-The-Box.

Wil Shriner

It's easy to identify people who can't count to ten. They're in front of you in the supermarket express lane.

M. Grundler

The trouble with our times is that the future is not what it used to be.

Paul Valéry

Too bad that all the people who know how to run the country are driving taxi cabs and cutting hair.

George Burns

The trouble with being punctual is that nobody's there to appreciate it.

Franklin P. Jones

I get furious with people who don't serve me immediately, if I think they're not doing anything.

If they're sort of closing drawers or checking lists or something, and they don't serve me immediately. I want to kill them. I want to leap over and throttle them.

Dillie Keane, Grumpy Old Women

The rage that happens in shops happens, normally, because of bad service. There's appalling service in Britain. Appalling. I mean unimaginably dire service, and we all put up with it.

India Knight, Grumpy Old Women

I am amazed at radio DJs today. I am firmly convinced that AM on my radio stands for Absolute Moron. I will not begin to tell you what FM stands for.

Jasper Carrott

We've all seen them, on the street corners, many of them smoking, many of them on drugs; they've got no jobs to go to, and once a week we see them queuing for the state hand-outs – or pensions, as we call them.

Harry Hill

What about safety matches? I never get that. What is a safety match? What does that mean? It's a box of matches you could ignite; you could burn a house down.

Nigel Havers, Grumpy Old Men

The Trouble Today is...

All my life I have sneered at the old farts who said that the world is going to the dogs, and at last I have realised, my God, they are right.

Jan Morris

Waiters and waitresses are becoming nicer and more caring. I used to pay my cheque, they would say, 'Thank you.' That's now escalated into, 'You take care of yourself, now.' The other day I paid my cheque and the waiter said, 'Don't put off that mammogram.'

Rita Rudner

...that it is all signpost and no destination.

Louis Kronenberger

The youth of the present day are quite monstrous. They have absolutely no respect for dyed hair.

Oscar Wilde

Newspapers are unable, seemingly, to discriminate between a bicycle accident and the collapse of civilisation.

George Bernard Shaw

You can say this for ready-mixes – the next generation isn't going to have any trouble making pies exactly like mother used to make.

Earl Wilson

The Trouble Today is...

We are living in a world today where lemonade is made from artificial flavours and furniture polish is made from real lemons.

Alfred E. Newman

You can find your way across this country using burger joints the way a navigator uses stars.

Charles Kuralt

Few cultures have not produced the idea that in some past era the world ran better than it does now.

Elizabeth Janeway

Now there are more overweight people in America than average-weight people. So overweight people are now average. Which means you've met your New Year's resolution.

Jay Leno

Pol Pot killed 1.7 million Cambodians, died under house arrest, well done there. Stalin killed many millions, died in his bed, aged 72, well done indeed. And the reason we let them get away with it is they killed their own people. And we're sort of fine with that. Hitler killed people next door. Oh, stupid man. After a couple of years we won't stand for that, will we?

Eddie Izzard

The Trouble Today is...

What some people mistake for the high cost of living is really the cost of high living.

Doug Larson

Nowadays men lead lives of noisy desperation.

James Thurber

If God had wanted us to vote, he would have given us candidates.

Jay Leno

The trouble with political jokes is that very often they get elected.

Will Rogers

The White House is giving George W. Bush intelligence briefings. You know, some of these jokes just write themselves.

David Letterman

My husband gave me a necklace. It's fake. I requested fake. Maybe I'm paranoid, but in this day and age, I don't want something around my neck that's worth more than my head.

Rita Rudner

Another possible source of guidance for teenagers is television, but television's message has always been that the need for truth, wisdom and world peace pales by comparison with the need for a toothpaste that offers whiter teeth and fresher breath.

Dave Barry

For the first time in history, sex is more dangerous than the cigarette afterward.

Jay Leno

I loathe the expression 'What makes him tick.' It is the American mind, looking for simple and singular solution, that uses the foolish expression. A person not only ticks, he also chimes and strikes the hour, falls and breaks and has to be put together again, and sometimes stops like an electric clock in a thunderstorm.

James Thurber

Politics: 'Poli', a Latin word meaning 'many'; and 'tics' meaning 'bloodsucking creatures'.

Robin Williams

Thus the metric system did not really catch on in the States, unless you count the increasing popularity of the nine-millimetre bullet.

Dave Barry

What the world needs is more geniuses with humility, there are so few of us left.

Oscar Levant

The Trouble Today is...

A common mistake people make when trying to design something completely foolproof is to underestimate the ingenuity of complete fools.

Douglas Adams

I have six locks on my door all in a row. When I go out, I only lock every other one. I figure no matter how long somebody stands there picking the locks, they are always locking three.

Elayne Boosler

It's amazing that the amount of news that happens in the world every day always just exactly fits the newspaper.

Jerry Seinfeld

For every fatal shooting, there were roughly three non-fatal shootings. And, folks, this is unacceptable in America. It's just unacceptable. And we're going to do something about it.

George W. Bush

Last week I was walking by a cemetery, two guys came after me with shovels. It was all about money.

Rodney Dangerfield

The streets are safe in Philadelphia. It's only the people who make them unsafe.

Frank Rizzo, ex-police chief and mayor of Philadelphia

Americans will put up with anything provided it doesn't block traffic.

Dan Rather

A bookstore is one of the only pieces of evidence we have that people are still thinking.

Jerry Seinfeld

I Don't Believe it!

GROANS AND GRIPES

In passing, also, I would like to say that the first time Adam had a chance he laid the blame on a woman.

Nancy Astor

Nothing is wrong with Southern California that a rise in the ocean level wouldn't cure.

Ross MacDonald

I hate the fact that [supermarkets are] supposed to be open 24 hours. What that means is if you go at ten at night, there's only one checkout open, so it takes you just as long as if you went at four o'clock in the afternoon.

Germaine Greer, Grumpy Old Women

There are three intolerable things in life – cold coffee, lukewarm champagne and overexcited women.

Orson Welles

I Don't Believe it!

My 50 years have shown me that few people know what they are talking about. I don't mean idiots that don't know. I mean everyone.

John Cleese

Every year, back comes Spring, with nasty little birds yapping their fool heads off and the ground all mucked up with plants.

Dorothy Parker

The vote means nothing to women. We should be armed.

Edna O'Brien

If all economists were laid end to end, they would not reach a conclusion.

George Bernard Shaw

Midlife can bring out your angry, bitter side. You look at your latte-swilling, beeper-wearing know-it-all teenager and think, 'For this I have stretch marks?'

Anon

I don't like small birds. They hop around so merrily outside my window, looking so innocent. But I know that secretly, they're watching my every move and plotting to beat me over the head with a large steel pipe and take my shoe.

Jack Handey

The countryside is incredibly boring. There's lots of shagging, lots of murders, lots of sarcasm, lots of treachery, and lots of bad cooking, but it's all hidden. You've got all the space and the flowers, but it's dull!

Tom Baker

If life were fair, Dan Quayle would be making a living asking 'Do you want fries with that?'

John Cleese

They'd go to the opening of an envelope. Any big occasion, they're always there. Anything for exposure. We can do without them.
Actors are unimportant.

Richard Harris

Getting old is a terrible thing, because in your head you're not… that's another reason for the grumpiness. You actually still think of yourself as 28, and you realise that people are kinda looking at you like a sad old boy. It's bloody annoying. I hate getting old.

Sir Gerry Robinson, Grumpy Old Men

There is a remarkable breakdown of taste and intelligence at Christmas time. Mature, responsible grown men wear neckties made of holly leaves and drink alcoholic beverages with raw egg yolks in them.

P.J. O'Rourke

I Don't Believe it!

When one door closes another one falls on top of you.

Angus Deayton

I tell you what really turns my toes up: love scenes with 68-year-old men and actresses young enough to be their granddaughter.

Mel Gibson

Potpourri. I even find the name irritating. Potpourri.

John O'Farrell, Grumpy Old Men

If you think health care is expensive now, wait until you see what it costs when it's free.

P.J. O'Rourke

The average airplane is 16 years old, and so is the average airplane meal.

Joan Rivers

If I were reincarnated, I would wish to be returned to Earth as a killer virus to lower human population levels.

Prince Philip

I have always hated that damn James Bond. I'd like to kill him.

Sean Connery

I am not over fond of animals.

David Attenborough

I think it's quite possible that there's a government department somewhere devoted to coming up with really annoying ideas. You know, let's not have fresh milk on trains any more, let's have those little cartons of UHT because that'll piss everyone off.

John O'Farrell, Grumpy Old Men

I have a total irreverence for anything connected with society except that which makes the roads safer, the beer stronger, the food cheaper and the old men and old women warmer in the winter and happier in the summer.

Brendan Behan

Why does a person even get up in the morning? You have breakfast, you floss your teeth so you'll have healthy gums in your old age, and then you get in your car and drive down I-10 and die. Life is so stupid I can't stand it.

Barbara Kingsolver

Progress might have been all right once, but it has gone on too long.

Ogden Nash

I wish people who have trouble communicating would just shut up.

Tom Lehrer

I Don't Believe it!

The surprising thing about young fools is how many survive to become old fools.

Doug Larson

I can win an argument on any topic, against any opponent. People know this, and steer clear of me at parties. Often, as a sign of their great respect, they don't even invite me.

Dave Barry

I don't have pet peeves, I have whole kennels of irritation.

Whoopi Goldberg

If life was fair, Elvis would be alive and all the impersonators would be dead.

Johnny Carson

I don't like animals. It's a strange thing, I don't like men and I don't like animals. As for God, he is beginning to disgust me.

Samuel Beckett

I hate women because they always know where things are.

James Thurber

If the English language made any sense, a catastrophe would be an apostrophe with fur.

Doug Larson

Think of how stupid the average person is, and realise half of them are stupider than that.

George Carlin

Santa Claus has the right idea. Visit people only once a year.

Victor Borge

Few things are more satisfying than seeing your own children have teenagers of their own.

Doug Larson

I don't like the word 'superstar'. It has ridiculous implications. These words – star, stupor, superstar, stupid star – they're misleading. It's a myth.

Barbra Streisand

I am so busy doing nothing… that the idea of doing anything – which as you know, always leads to something – cuts into the nothing and then forces me to have to drop everything.

Jerry Seinfeld

I'm getting fed up of living away from home so much. They look after you very well but it doesn't matter how well you're looked after, how nice the hotel is, if you're away from home constantly, the bloody dog savages you, thinks you're a stranger, the kid cries and the wife's stuck to your face!

David Jason

I Don't Believe it!

USA Today has come out with a new survey: apparently three out of four people make up 75 per cent of the population.

David Letterman

Women speak because they wish to speak, whereas a man speaks only when driven to speech by something outside himself – like, for instance, he can't find any clean socks.

Jean Kerr

Now they show you how detergents take out bloodstains, a pretty violent image there. I think if you've got a T-shirt with a bloodstain all over it, maybe laundry isn't your biggest problem. Maybe you should get rid of the body before you do the wash.

Jerry Seinfeld

Rock journalism is people who can't write interviewing people who can't talk for people who can't read.

Frank Zappa

If the world should blow itself up, the last audible voice would be that of an expert saying it can't be done.

Peter Ustinov

I think on-stage nudity is disgusting, shameful and damaging to all things American. But if I were 22 with a great body, it would be artistic, tasteful, patriotic and a progressive religious experience.

Shelley Winters

Man invented language to satisfy his deep need to complain.

Lily Tomlin

The days of the digital watch are numbered.

Tom Stoppard

A healthy male adult bore consumes each year one and a half times his own weight in other people's patience.

John Updike

I'm convinced there's a small room in the attic of the Foreign Office where future diplomats are taught to stammer.

Peter Ustinov

A lot of people like snow. I find it to be an unnecessary freezing of water.

Carl Reiner

An intellectual snob is someone who can listen to the William Tell Overture and not think of *The Lone Ranger*.

Dan Rather

Life is a Cruise

My parents didn't want to move to Florida, but they turned 60, and that's the law.

Jerry Seinfeld

I love flying. I've been to almost as many places as my luggage.

Bob Hope

You haven't lived until you've died in California.

Mort Sahl

They invented the three-day bank holiday weekend because you can't lump all the bad weather into just Saturday and Sunday.

Anon

The great and recurring question about abroad is, is it worth getting there?

Rose Macaulay

Abroad is unutterably bloody and foreigners are fiends.

Nancy Mitford

The scientific theory I like best is that the rings of Saturn are composed entirely of lost airline luggage.

Mark Russell

I don't hold with abroad and think foreigners speak English when our backs are turned.

Quentin Crisp

I wouldn't mind seeing China if I could come back the same day.

Philip Larkin

I hate vacations. There's nothing to do.

David Mamet

I also hate those holidays that fall on a Monday where you don't get mail, those fake holidays like Columbus Day. What did Christopher Columbus do, discover America? If he hadn't, somebody else would have and we'd still be here. Big deal.

John Waters

I said I didn't want to spend most of my life in Holidays Inns, but I've checked and they've all been redecorated. They're marvellous places to stay and I've thought it over and that's where I'd like to be.

Walter F. Mondale

Some national parks have long waiting lists for camping reservations. When you have to wait a year to sleep next to a tree, something is wrong.

George Carlin

Meat and Two Veg

When you get to 52 food becomes more important than sex.

Prue Leith

Everything I eat has been proved by some doctor or other to be a deadly poison, and everything I don't eat has been proved to be indispensable for life. But I go marching on.

George Bernard Shaw

I've decided to make Granny Moon's Sheep's Head Soup. Don't worry, the name's a bit misleading. It's actually more of a stew.

Daphne Moon, Frasier

When men reach their 60s and retire they go to pieces. Women just go right on cooking.

Gail Sheehy

I refuse to spend my life worrying about what I eat. There is no pleasure worth forgoing just for an extra three years in the geriatric ward.

John Mortimer

I don't like food that's too carefully arranged; it makes me think that the chef is spending too much time arranging and not enough time cooking. If I wanted a picture I'd buy a painting.

Andy Rooney

I just love Chinese food. My favourite dish is number 27.

Clement Attlee

My friend, Lily, can recognise 157 different cheeses just by looking at the labels.

Mrs. Merton

Once, during prohibition, I was forced to live for days on nothing but food and water.

W.C. Fields

My doctor told me to stop having intimate dinners for four; unless there are three other people.

Orson Welles

A fruit is a vegetable with looks and money. Plus, if you let fruit rot, it turns into wine; something Brussels sprouts never do.

P.J. O'Rourke

I am a bit of a dictator when it comes to mealtimes. They have to eat their vegetables. They kick and scream to start with but if you persist they will eventually come round to your way of thinking. Now, a Brussels sprout is quite welcome in the family.

Antony Worrall Thompson

The English contribution to world cuisine – the chip.

John Cleese

It is inhumane, in my opinion, to force people who have a genuine medical need for coffee to wait in line behind people who apparently view it as some kind of recreational activity.

Dave Barry

Another teatime, another day older.

Jethro Tull

The funny thing about Thanksgiving, or any huge meal, is that you spend 12 hours shopping for it and then chopping and cooking and braising and blanching. Then it takes 20 minutes to eat it and everybody sort of sits around in a food coma, and then it takes four hours to clean it up.

Ted Allen

A wasp in an ice cube? What next? Dog turd on a cocktail stick?

Victor Meldrew

I will not eat oysters. I want my food dead. Not sick, not wounded, dead.

Woody Allen

Coffee in England always tastes like a chemistry experiment.

Agatha Christie

Ageing is when you hear 'snap, crackle, pop' before you get to breakfast.

Anon

It was a bold man who first swallowed an oyster.

Jonathan Swift

I don't cook any more. No one in their right mind does. People complain that young people no longer know how to, but I say good. No one weaves their own cloth these days either.

Shirley Conran

Kissing don't last; cookery do!

George Meredith

Cooking is like love. It should be entered into with abandon or not at all.

Harriet Van Horne

It's difficult to think anything but pleasant thoughts while eating a home-grown tomato.

Lewis Grizzard

High-tech tomatoes. Mysterious milk. Supersquash. Are we supposed to eat this stuff? Or is it going to eat us?

Annita Manning

I would like to find a stew that will give me heartburn immediately, instead of at three o'clock in the morning.

John Barrymore

Ask not what you can do for your country. Ask what's for lunch.

Orson Welles

One of the very nicest things about life is the way we must regularly stop whatever it is we are doing and devote our attention to eating.

Luciano Pavarotti and William Wright, Pavarotti, My Own Story

What I say is that, if a man really likes potatoes, he must be a pretty decent sort of fellow.

A.A. Milne

I come from a family where gravy is considered a beverage.

Erma Bombeck

My idea of heaven is eating pâté de foie gras to the sound of trumpets.

Sydney Smith

Spaghetti can be eaten most successfully if you inhale it like a vacuum cleaner.

Sophia Loren

The only time to eat diet food is while you're waiting for the steak to cook.

Julia Child

People say fish is good for a diet. But fish should never be cooked in butter. Fish should be cooked in its natural oils – Texaco, Mobil, Exxon…

Rodney Dangerfield

Grandparents Know Best

At heart, I suspect she would like nothing better than to let go of the facelifts and dieting and settle down to blissful grannyhood.

Julia Llewellyn Smith, on Joan Rivers

If I had known my grandchildren would be so much fun I would have had them first!

Anon

My grandfather once told me that there were two kinds of people: those who do the work and those who take the credit. He told me to try to be in the first group; there was much less competition.

Indira Gandhi

I am playing grandmothers in movies now.

Raquel Welch

Grandparents Know Best

My grandmother has a bumper sticker on her car that says, 'Sexy Senior Citizen.' You don't want to think of your grandmother that way, do you? Out entering wet shawl contests. Makes you wonder where she got that dollar she gave you for your birthday.

Andy Rooney

It's amazing how grandparents seem so young once you become one.

Anon

My grandmother took a bath every year, whether she needed it or not.

Brendan Behan

Grandchildren are God's way of compensating us for growing old.

Mary H. Waldrip

An hour with your grandchildren can make you feel young again. Anything longer than that, and you start to age quickly.

Gene Perret

No cowboy was ever faster on the draw than a grandparent pulling a baby picture out of a wallet.

Anon

If God had intended us to follow recipes, He wouldn't have given us grandmothers.

Linda Henley

The best baby-sitters, of course, are the baby's grandparents. You feel completely comfortable entrusting your baby to them for long periods, which is why most grandparents flee to Florida.

Dave Barry

My granddaughter came to spend a few weeks with me, and I decided to teach her to sew. After I had gone through a lengthy explanation of how to thread the machine, she stepped back, put her hands on her hips, and said in disbelief, 'You mean you can do all that, but you can't play my Game Boy?'

Anon

'You're more trouble than the children are' is the greatest compliment a grandparent can receive.

Gene Perret

Technophobes and Technophiles

Unlike most women of my generation I do love computers, but I get terribly angry when it freezes, you know, it freezes and sends you messages saying you have committed an illegal action. Sorry, I am sitting here minding my own business. I have done nothing wrong. It's you that has frozen. Something has gone wrong in your innards. How dare you blame me?

Sheila Hancock, Grumpy Old Women

Technophobes and Technophiles

How can I believe in God when just last week I
got my tongue caught in the roller of an electric
typewriter?

Woody Allen

Computers are useless. They can only give you
answers.

Pablo Picasso

Television is chewing gum for the eyes.

Frank Lloyd Wright

I am not the only person who uses his computer
mainly for the purpose of diddling with his
computer.

Dave Barry

It is only when they go wrong that machines
remind you how powerful they are.

Clive James

The thing with high-tech is that you always end
up using scissors.

David Hockney

I get in a complete rage with the computer. I get
all hot, my hair is standing on end, I look like a
clown trying to control myself... Then I get up
and walk away and the bloody egg-timer on the
screen is still there.

Nina Myskow, Grumpy Old Women

Technophobes and Technophiles

In view of all the deadly computer viruses that have been spreading lately, *Weekend Update* would like to remind you: when you link up to another computer, you're linking up to every computer that that computer has ever linked up to.

Dennis Miller

Technology frightens me to death. It's designed by engineers to impress other engineers, and they always come with instruction booklets that are written by engineers for other engineers – which is why almost no technology ever works.

John Cleese

You switch off and reboot and all this sort of thing. I tell you, I have felt sometimes like opening up the window and hurling my computer out, and the only reason I don't do so is concern for the people down below. Because if you're going to be brained, please not by a computer.

Ann Widdecombe, Grumpy Old Women

Oh, they have the Internet on computers now.

Homer Simpson

I hate television. I hate it as much as peanuts. But I can't stop eating peanuts.

Orson Welles

Technophobes and Technophiles

If it weren't for electricity, we'd all be watching television by candlelight.

George Gobel

It was not so long ago that people thought semiconductors were part-time orchestra leaders and microchips were very, very small snack foods.

Geraldine Ferraro

All I need now is a computer. And a 10-year-old kid to teach me how to use it.

Chevy Chase, Fletch Lives

I'm glad cave-people didn't invent television, because they would have just sat around and watched talk shows all day instead of creating tools.

Dave James

I think there is a world market for maybe five computers.

Thomas Watson, Chairman of IBM, 1943

I find television very educating. Every time somebody turns on the set, I go into the other room and read a book.

Groucho Marx

Technophobes and Technophiles

If it weren't for Philo T. Farnsworth, inventor of the television, we'd still be eating frozen radio dinners.

Johnny Carson

Home computers are being called upon to perform many new functions, including the consumption of homework formerly eaten by the dog.

Doug Larson

Her own mother lived the latter years of her life in the horrible suspicion that electricity was dripping invisibly all over the house.

James Thurber

Buying the right computer and getting it to work properly is no more complicated than building a nuclear reactor from wristwatch parts in a darkened room using only your teeth.

Dave Barry

I've thrown three mobile phones into the Thames in the past because I couldn't work them. I've never been on the Internet in my life. My wife Barbara gave me a computer but I haven't a clue how to work it.

Rik Mayall

Technophobes and Technophiles

I love technology. Matches, to light a fire is really
high-tech. The wheel is really one of the great
inventions of all time. Other than that I am an
ignoramus about technology. I once looked for the
'ON' button on the computer and came to find
out it was on the back. Then I thought, anyone
who would put the 'ON' switch on the back,
where you can't find it, doesn't do any good for my
psyche. The one time I did get the computer on, I
couldn't turn the damn thing off!

William Shatner

I don't care if people think I'm a dumb blonde,
or stupid or an average actress or over the hill.
I'm gonna have a very successful Internet
company and I'm gonna have $100 million in the
bank and I don't really give a sh★t what anybody
thinks.

Melanie Griffith

A new Viagra virus is going round the Internet. It
doesn't affect your hard drive, but you can't
minimise anything for hours.

Joan Rivers

Every time you think television has hit its lowest
ebb, a new programme comes along to make you
wonder where you thought the ebb was.

Art Buchwald

Television is more interesting than people. If it were not we should have people standing in the corner of our room.

Alan Coren

Old Father Time

This is your life and it's ending one minute at a time.

David Fincher

Time is a great teacher, but unfortunately it kills all its pupils.

Hector Berlioz

I have decided that Father Time doesn't come after everybody with a scythe. He has come to me often with a pair of tweezers – he takes a little nip here and then a little nip there and I'm sure that eventually he'll have all of me.

Anon

Tobacco, coffee, alcohol, hashish, prussic acid, strychnine, are weak dilutions: the surest poison is time.

Ralph Waldo Emerson

Old Father Time

Those of you in your 20s have the feeling that time is something of which you have an endless supply. Again, take it from someone who has been on this planet a good deal longer than most of you have, that is not the case.

Chief Justice William H. Rehnquist

Senescence begins and middle age ends the day your descendants outnumber your friends.

Ogden Nash

You can't leave footprints in the sands of time if you're sitting on your butt. And who wants to leave butt-prints in the sands of time?

Anon

I want to go ahead of Father Time with a scythe of my own.

H. G. Wells

Every girl should use what Mother Nature gave her before Father Time takes it away.

Laurence J. Peter

Yes, time flies. And where did it leave you? Old too soon… smart too late.

Mike Tyson

Life is...

...like a sewer. What you get out of it depends on what you put into it.

Tom Lehrer

...like a play: it's not the length, but the excellence of the acting that matters.

Seneca

...the art of drawing without an eraser.

Anon

...the art of drawing sufficient conclusions from insufficient data.

Samuel Butler

...a sexually transmitted disease and the mortality rate is 100 per cent.

R.D. Laing

...something that happens when you can't get to sleep.

Fran Lebowitz

...hard. After all, it kills you.

Katharine Hepburn

...like playing a violin solo in public and learning the instrument as one goes on.

Samuel Butler

Life is...

...a tragedy when seen in close-up, but a comedy in long-shot.

Charlie Chaplin

...a long lesson in humility.

James M. Barrie

...like a taxi. The meter just keeps a-ticking whether you are getting somewhere or just standing still.

Lou Erickso

...a succession of lessons which must be lived to be understood.

Ralph Waldo Emerson

...wasted on the living.

Douglas Adams

...like a roll of toilet paper; long and useful, but it always ends at the wrong moment.

Anon

Life can be wildly tragic at times, and I've had my share. But whatever happens to you, you have to keep a slightly comic attitude. In the final analysis, you have got not to forget to laugh.

Katharine Hepburn

What you have to do in life is not look back at all
the grievances but look forward to what is ahead.

Terry Waite

All I can say about life is, Oh God, enjoy it!

Bob Newhart

He felt that his whole life was some kind of dream
and he sometimes wondered whose it was and
whether they were enjoying it.

Douglas Adams

I hope life isn't a big joke, because I don't get it.

Jack Handey

I long ago came to the conclusion that all life is six
to five against.

Damon Runyon

You suddenly realise that life moves at an
incredible speed. When I take my granddaughter
to Hampstead Heath I go to the same places I
used to take her father. It just seems that life has
telescoped.

Anon

The evening of a well-spent life brings its lamps
with it.

Joseph Joubert

The average man, who does not know what to do with his life, wants another one which will last forever.

Anatole France

Meet Your Maker

I don't want to achieve immortality through my work, I want to achieve it through not dying.

Woody Allen

There are three natural anaesthetics: sleep, fainting, and death.

Oliver Wendell Holmes

Tears are sometimes an inappropriate response to death. When a life has been lived completely honestly, completely successfully, or just completely, the correct response to death's perfect punctuation mark is a smile.

Julie Burchill

Death is just nature's way of telling you to slow down.

Dick Sharples

The fear of death is the most unjustified of all fears, for there's no risk of accident for someone who's dead.

Albert Einstein

Death is the greatest kick of all – that's why they save it till last.

Graffito

The closing years of life are like the end of a masquerade party, when the masks are dropped.

Arthur Schopenhauer

The world is getting to be such a dangerous place, a guy is lucky to get out of it alive.

W.C. Fields

What's death like? It's as bad as the chicken at Tresky's Restaurant.

Woody Allen

When I die, I want it to be on my hundredth birthday, in my beach house on Maui, and I want my husband to be so upset he has to drop out of college.

Roz Doyle, Frasier

Life is pleasant. Death is peaceful.
It's the transition that's troublesome.

Isaac Asimov

I'd rather be dead than singing 'Satisfaction' when I'm 45.

Mick Jagger

Meet Your Maker

I enjoy life. I think I'll enjoy death even more.

Cat Stevens

I wanted to be bored to death, as good a way to go as any.

Peter DeVries

One thing about being successful is that I stopped being afraid of dying. Once you're a star you're dead already. You're embalmed.

Dustin Hoffman

The report of my death was an exaggeration.

Mark Twain

I'd hate to die twice. It's so boring.

Richard P. Feynman

Dying is easy. Comedy is difficult.

Edmund Gwenn

The idea is to die young as late as possible.

Ashley Montagu

It's funny how most people love the dead, once you're dead you're made for life.

Jimi Hendrix

I fear vastly more a futile, incompetent old age than I do any form of death.

William Allen White

I don't believe in dying. It's been done. I'm working on a new exit.

George Burns

Everyone is afraid of dying alone. I don't understand. Who wants to die and have to be polite at the same time?

Quentin Crisp

The first sign of his approaching end was when one of my old aunts, when undressing him, removed a toe with one of his socks.

Graham Greene

Death will be a great relief. No more interviews.

Katharine Hepburn

Everybody has got to die but I have always believed an exception would be made in my case.

William Saroyan

First thing I do when I wake up in the morning is breathe on the mirror and hope it fogs.

Earl Wynn

Meet Your Maker

I can't die. It would ruin my image.

Jack LaLanne

If you die in an elevator, be sure to push the up button.

Sam Levenson

My father passed away very quietly in his sleep… between the bar and the gents.

Barry Humphries

Death is a low chemical trick played on everybody except sequoia trees.

J.J. Furnas

I'm not afraid of death. It's the makeover at the undertaker's that scares me…They try to make you look as lifelike as possible, which defeats the whole purpose. It's hard to feel bad for somebody who looks better than you do.

Anita Wise

The difference between sex and death is that with death you can do it alone and no one is going to make fun of you.

Woody Allen

Eternity is a terrible thought. I mean, where's it going to end?

Tom Stoppard

If I could drop dead right now, I'd be the happiest man alive.

Samuel Goldwyn

The only completely consistent people are the dead.

Aldous Huxley

I don't think kids have a problem with death. It's us older ones who are nearer to it that start being frightened.

Helena Bonham Carter

Don't be afraid your life will end; be afraid that it will never begin.

Grace Hansen

Dying doesn't frighten me in the slightest though I should love to see my grandchildren grow up, but I don't want to get old and infirm and not be able to enjoy my life.

Beryl Bainbridge

I know a woman who had her husband cremated and then mixed his ashes with grass and smoked him. She said it was the best he'd made her feel in years.

Maureen Murphy

Meet Your Maker

Once the game is over, the king and the pawn go back in the same box.

Italian proverb

I'm the one that's got to die when it's time for me to die, so let me live my life the way I want to.

Jimi Hendrix

He who dies with the most toys is, nonetheless, still dead.

Anon

Either he's dead or my watch has stopped.

Groucho Marx

It's impossible to experience one's death objectively and still carry a tune.

Woody Allen

In the end, everything is a gag.

Charlie Chaplin

To lose one parent may be regarded as a misfortune; to lose both looks like carelessness.

Oscar Wilde

I wouldn't mind dying – it's the business of having to stay dead that scares the sh★t out of me.

R. Geis

With the newspaper strike on, I wouldn't consider dying.

Bette Davis, on being told that her death was rumoured

Death would be a beautiful place if it looks like Brad Pitt.

Carmen Electra

When it comes time to die, be not like those whose hearts are filled with the fear of death, so when their time comes they weep and pray for a little more time to live their lives over again in a different way. Sing your death song, and die like a hero going home.

Mohican Chief Aupumut

If my doctor told me I had only six minutes to live, I wouldn't brood. I'd type a little faster.

Isaac Asimov

When I die I want to decompose in a barrel of porter and have it served in all the pubs in Ireland.

J. P. Donleavy, The Ginger Man

My young son asked me what happens after we die. I told him we get buried under a bunch of dirt and worms eat our bodies. I guess I should have told him the truth – that most of us go to Hell and burn eternally – but I didn't want to upset him.

Jack Handey

Meet Your Maker

Every man of genius is considerably helped by being dead.

Robert Lynd

Alas, I am dying beyond my means.

Oscar Wilde

My grandmother made dying her life's work.

Hugh Leonard

I would never die for my beliefs because I might be wrong.

Bertrand Russell

Sure there have been injuries and deaths in boxing – but none of them serious.

Alan Minter

There's something about death that is comforting, the thought that you could die tomorrow frees you to appreciate your life now.

Angelina Jolie

Life does not cease to be funny when people die any more than it ceases to be serious when people laugh.

George Bernard Shaw

When I die, just keep playing the records.

Jimi Hendrix

Heavens Above or Hell Below?

Everybody wants to go to Heaven, but nobody wants to die.

Joe Louis

In Heaven all the interesting people are missing.

Friedrich Nietzsche

The Devil himself had probably re-designed Hell in the light of information he had gained from observing airport layouts.

Anthony Price

...to be in a crowded theatre with lots of old people is quite frightening. Surrounded by men in tartan trousers and bifocals and women whose last orgasm coincided with the Suez crises, it was like being in the waiting room for heaven.

Gareth McLean

When did I realise I was God? Well, I was praying and I suddenly realised I was talking to myself.

Peter O'Toole

And God said, 'Let there be light' and there was light, but the Electricity Board said He would have to wait until Thursday to be connected.

Spike Milligan

Heavens Above or Hell Below?

Maybe there is no actual place called Hell. Maybe Hell is just having to listen to our grandparents breathe through their noses when they're eating sandwiches.

Jim Carrey

If you're going through Hell, keep going.

Sir Winston Churchill

What! You been keeping records on me? I wasn't so bad! How many times did I take the Lord's name in vain? One million and six! Jesus Ch...!

Steve Martin

I can't stand light. I hate weather. My idea of Heaven is moving from one smoke-filled room to another.

Peter O'Toole

When we drink, we get drunk. When we get drunk, we fall asleep. When we fall asleep, we commit no sin. When we commit no sin, we go to Heaven. So, let's all get drunk and go to Heaven!

Brian O'Rourke

When I die, I hope to go to Heaven, whatever the Hell that is.

Ayn Rand

There is no Hell. There is only France.

Frank Zappa

What a pity Hell's gates are not kept by O'Flynn
The surly old dog would let nobody in.

Patrick Ireland, on the epitaph of an Irish security guard

God is love. I have loved. Therefore, I will go to
heaven.

Imelda Marcos

Hell is full of musical amateurs.

George Bernard Shaw

Last Laughs and Epitaphs

My uncle Sammy was an angry man. He had
printed on his tombstone: What are you looking
at?

Margaret Smith

A damn good funeral is still one of our best and
cheapest acts of theatre.

Gwyn Thomas

My luck is so bad that if I bought a cemetery,
people would stop dying.

Ed Furgol

Last Laughs and Epitaphs

When I have one foot in the grave, I will tell the whole truth about women. I shall tell it, jump into my coffin, pull the lid over me and say, 'Do what you like now.'

Leo Tolstoy

My grandfather was a very insignificant man, actually. At his funeral his hearse followed the other cars.

Woody Allen

Here lies the body of Mary Ann Lowder.
She burst while drinking a seltzer powder.
Called from the world to her heavenly rest,
She should have waited till it effervesced.

Anon

In India when a man dies, his widow throws herself on the funeral pyre. Over here, she says, 'Fifty ham baps, Beryl – you slice, I'll butter.'

Victoria Wood

There's no such thing as bad publicity except your own obituary.

Brendan Behan

When I am dead, I hope it may be said: 'His sins were scarlet but his books were read.'

Hilaire Belloc

Last Laughs and Epitaphs

Here lies Jan Smith, wife of Thomas Smith, Marble Cutter. This monument was erected by her husband as a tribute to her memory and a specimen of his work. Monuments of this same style are $250.

Gravestone inscription

Son: Do you want to be buried, Mum? Or shall we have you cremated?
Mother: Oh, I don't know, love. Surprise me!

Deric Longden

Edina: No, no, no grave for me, sweetie. I'm a Buddhist anyway. I want to be lain out on a rock in the middle of the Ganges, darling, and then just pecked by birds. I don't want to end up as some drugged-up zombie in a hospital, all right?
Saffie: I thought that would appeal to you…

Absolutely Fabulous

This is on me.

Dorothy Parker, suggestion for her tombstone

She did it the hard way.

Bette Davis's epitaph

Called back.

Emily Dickinson's epitaph

Last Laughs and Epitaphs

Here lies W.C. Fields. I would rather be living in Philadelphia.

> *W.C. Fields's* suggestion for his epitaph
> to *Vanity Fair* in 1925

I always remember an epitaph which is in the cemetery at Tombstone, Arizona. It says: 'Here lies Jack Williams. He done his damnedest.' I think that is the greatest epitaph a man can have.

> *Harry S. Truman*

Over my dead body!

> *George S. Kaufman,* suggested epitaph

A funeral eulogy is a belated plea for the defence delivered after the evidence is all in.

> *Irvin S. Cobb*

When I die, my epitaph should read: She Paid the Bills. That's the story of my private life.

> *Gloria Swanson*

May my husband rest in peace till I get there.

> *Dame Edna Everage*

Everybody loves you when you're six foot in the ground.

> *John Lennon*

I was terrible at straight items. When I wrote obituaries, my mother said the only thing I ever got them to do was die in alphabetical order.

Erma Bombeck

When you've told someone that you've left them a legacy the only decent thing to do is to die at once.

Samuel Butler

I wish to be cremated. One tenth of my ashes shall be given to my agent, as written in our contract.

Groucho Marx

Never say you know a person until you have divided an inheritance with them.

Johann Lavater

Famous Last Words

Bless you, Sister. May all your sons be bishops.

Brendan Behan

Why not? After all, it belongs to him.

Charlie Chaplin, after a priest said, 'May the Lord have mercy on your soul.'

Never felt better.

Douglas Fairbanks Snr.

Famous Last Words

That was a great game of golf, fellers.

Harry Lillis 'Bing' Crosby

God damn the whole friggin' world but you,
Carlotta.

W.C. Fields

On the contrary.

Henrik Ibsen, after hearing a nurse remark
that he was feeling better

This is it! I'm going. I'm going.

Al Jolson

Bugger Bognor

George V, having been assured by his physician that he
would soon be fit enough to holiday in Bognor Regis

Why not? Yeah. Beautiful.

Timothy Leary

Is everybody happy? I want everybody to be happy.
I know I'm happy.

Ethel Barrymore

Go on, get out! Last words are for fools who
haven't said enough!

Karl Marx

Why should I talk to you? I've just been talking to your boss.

> *Wilson Mizner*, to a priest standing over his bed

Born in a hotel room and, goddamn it, died in a hotel room.

> *Eugene O'Neill*

Drink to me!

> *Pablo Picasso*

God bless… God damn.

> *James Thurber*

Go away. I'm all right.

> *H. G. Wells*

Curtain! Fast music! Lights! Ready for the last finale! Great! The show looks good. The show looks good.

> *Florenz Ziegfeld*, Broadway producer

Die? I should say not, dear fellow. No Barrymore would allow such a conventional thing to happen to him.

> *John Barrymore*

Friends applaud, the comedy is finished.

> *Ludwig van Beethoven*

Famous Last Words

I am about to – or I am going to – die: either expression is correct.

Dominique Bouhours, French grammarian

Goodnight, my darlings, I'll see you tomorrow.

Noel Coward

Why do you weep? Did you think I was immortal?

Louis XIV, King of France

Sister, you're trying to keep me alive as an old curiosity, but I'm done, I'm finished, I'm going to die.

George Bernard Shaw, to his nurse

Oh, I am not going to die, am I? He will not separate us, we have been so happy.

Charlotte Brontë, to her husband of nine months, Rev. Arthur Nicholls

I've had 18 straight whiskies, I think that's the record…

Dylan Thomas

I should never have switched from Scotch to Martinis.

Humphrey Bogart

I've had a hell of a lot of fun and I've enjoyed every minute of it.

Errol Flynn

I have offended God and mankind because my work did not reach the quality it should have.

Leonardo da Vinci

My wallpaper and I are fighting a duel to the death. One or the other of us has to go.

Oscar Wilde

This isn't *Hamlet*, you know, it's not meant to go into the bloody ear.

Laurence Olivier, to his nurse, who had spilt water on him

Dammit… Don't you dare ask God to help me.

Joan Crawford, after her housekeeper began to pray aloud

This is absurd!

Sigmund Freud

I'd rather be skiing than doing what I'm doing.

Stan Laurel

It's all been rather lovely.

John Le Mesurier

Die, my dear doctor? That's the last thing I shall do.

Lord Palmerston

Famous Last Words

If this is dying, I don't think much of it.

Lytton Strachey

I'll always remember the last words of my grandfather, 'A truck!'

Emo Philips

Index

Index

Index

Index

Index

Index

Index

Index

Index